DRAGON RISING

DRAGON RISING

KATIE & KEVIN TSANG

SIMON & SCHUSTER

First published in Great Britain in 2022 by Simon & Schuster UK Ltd

Copyright © 2022 Katherine Webber Tsang and Kevin Tsang

1 3 5 7 9 10 8 6 4 2

Simon & Schuster UK Ltd
1st Floor, 222 Gray's Inn Road
London WC1X 8HB

www.simonandschuster.co.uk
www.simonandschuster.com.au
www.simonandschuster.co.in

Simon & Schuster Australia, Sydney
Simon & Schuster India, New Delhi

A CIP catalogue record for this book
is available from the British Library.

PB ISBN 978-1-3985-0590-2
eBook ISBN 978-1-3985-0591-9
eAudio ISBN 978-1-3985-0592-6

Typeset in Garamond by M Rules
Printed and bound by CPI Group (UK) Ltd, Croydon, CR0 4YY

For our daughters

The Sea

The sea is full of mysteries. You never know what you might find hidden in its depths. Lying between the earth and sky, the sea is always moving, with secrets dwelling deep below. Waves crash on the shore, tides go in and out, but even when the sea looks still, the currents race and dance beneath the surface. The sea is an in-between place. And like anywhere in-between, it holds more than meets the eye.

Deep below the surface, down where it is cold and dark, there is a sudden explosion of light and energy. A creature emerges, roaring with confusion and alarm.

It does not know where it is.

All it knows is that it must get to the surface. It must find what it seeks.

It swims and swims through the sea, through that in-between space, and, up above, nobody knows that everything has changed.

Blast at the Beach

Billy Chan missed his dragon.

It had been three weeks since he'd returned home to California. His three best friends that he'd met at summer camp had all gone back to their respective homes and now they were scattered around the world: Billy in San Francisco, Charlotte Bell in Atlanta, Dylan O'Donnell in Galway and Liu Ling-Fei in a small village in China outside Camp Dragon. That was where their adventure had first begun.

More recently they had defeated the Dragon of Death for good in Dragon City and returned to Camp Dragon, where they'd had the best summer ever. It was good to be back in their own time, in their own world, after being sucked into a terrifying alternate future where the Dragon of Death ruled over humans and dragons alike. Billy sometimes imagined a world in which humans and dragons lived together in peace, but it didn't look anything like Dragon City. He still had nightmares about that place and what might have happened if they hadn't defeated the Dragon of Death.

After surviving the perils of Dragon City, and everything that had come before, Billy had known how lucky they were to be together, and to be back at Camp Dragon. And they'd still had their dragons, even if they'd been on the other side of the mountain. They had sneaked out to visit them through the mountain as often as they could, but the friends had also had fun at camp. Swimming in the lake, learning martial arts and trying new food in cooking class had been how they filled their days. Even the Mandarin language lessons hadn't been too bad. But the best part had been being all together, and knowing their dragons were safe and free once more. For the first time all summer, Billy had felt carefree, as if he could just be a kid.

Well, a kid who had his very own dragon. But that only made things better.

Since Old Gold, who had run Camp Dragon when they'd first arrived, had been banished into a black hole with the Dragon of Death, there was now a new camp director. She was kind and fun and exactly what you would hope for in someone running a summer camp. And she certainly didn't have any secret evil plans like Old Gold. He had originally set up Camp Dragon to locate the children who were the key to opening the mountain behind the camp and uncovering mythical dragons.

Despite everything, Billy couldn't hate Old Gold. After all, if he'd never started Camp Dragon, Billy never would have met Charlotte, Dylan and Ling-Fei. He never would have heart-bonded with Spark.

A heart bond was an ancient and rare connection forged between a human and a dragon who had matching hearts, and once the bond was made it could not be broken. Each of the four children had heart-bonded with a different dragon, and not only did the dragons have increased power and ability thanks to the heart bond, the children also gained a unique power. Billy couldn't imagine life without his dragon. That was part of the reason he was having such a hard time adapting back to normal life.

He'd come home to California with new friends, improved Mandarin skills (which was why his parents had sent him to camp in the first place) and a humongous secret. The Billy who had arrived at Camp Dragon at the start of summer had morphed into a new Billy. His parents kept commenting on how much more mature he seemed. How much more confident. But they'd noticed he'd withdrawn from his old friends and preferred to spend his time surfing or in his room talking to Charlotte, Dylan and Ling-Fei online. Billy couldn't help it – he felt as if he had so much less in common with his friends from his life before camp. The things they worried about seemed silly to him now. He felt as if Charlotte, Dylan and Ling-Fei were the only ones who understood him. And Spark, of course.

'We know you miss your friends from camp,' Billy's mom had said. 'But right now you have to focus on getting ready for school to start.'

'You can all meet up at camp again next year,' his dad had added.

Billy had known there was nothing he could do or say to convince them that these new friends were so much more than friends. That without them, he wouldn't have survived the summer. That without them, he couldn't have saved the world. He had heart-bonded with his dragon, but he had a special bond with Charlotte, Dylan and Ling-Fei too, because of what they'd been through together. A bond almost as unbreakable as his bond with Spark. Sometimes he couldn't quite believe that it had all really happened, but having his friends in his life made it real. After his family, they were the most important people to him. So instead he had just nodded and tried to remember what life had been like before.

But every morning when Billy went surfing, he wished that he were riding a dragon instead of a wave. Surfing almost felt like flying. It took patience, but it was always worth the wait when he caught the perfect wave. Before Billy had ever ridden a dragon, he'd thought it was the closest he'd come to flying. Now he knew better.

There was a small, secret cove that he'd recently discovered and it was the perfect place for early morning surfing. The only way to reach it was on foot, down narrow trails winding along steep cliffs.

His parents didn't know that was where he surfed and Billy knew they would almost certainly forbid him if they found out. They thought he went down to the main beach, where there were other people around if he needed help. They didn't know that he had faced far scarier things than waves and survived to tell the tale. But Billy didn't want to be around other people. He might have wanted to share the beach, and the secret of what had happened this summer, with his brother, Eddie, but he had already gone back to university for a summer course, so Billy was left with his own thoughts. He didn't mind too much though. He liked being out alone on the waves, where he felt the most connected to Spark. There was something about being in nature that made him feel closer to his dragon. When he was floating in the ocean, overwhelmed by how vast and powerful it was, it reminded him of the dragons. It gave him the same sense of awe. He'd always loved the water, but now it drew him more and more, connecting him with his dragon who was far away in the Dragon Realm.

Billy had grown used to the ache that came from being separated from his dragon, the dragon that he was heart-bonded to for ever. It felt like a dull pain now, always there, but easy to ignore. And it was worth it to know he was still connected to Spark, even across the realms.

There'd been only once when he hadn't been able to sense her, and that was when she had betrayed Billy and the others and joined the Dragon of Death. Their heart bond hadn't truly broken, only death could sever it, but when Spark's heart had darkened, she had blocked their connection. It had been awful. He'd felt as if he'd lost a piece of himself.

At least now, even with Spark far away in another realm, he could still reach her through their bond. The distance meant that her responses were delayed, but it was better than nothing. They used to be able to communicate instantly in their minds; now it felt more like sending telegrams. Billy didn't know how long it would take for his messages to reach Spark. Sometimes it was hours before he had a response from her and sometimes even days. He knew why it took longer now, but it still made him anxious. He couldn't help but worry that one day he'd try to reach her and she wouldn't be there.

But then he would remind himself that there was no point in worrying about things he couldn't control. Surfing helped with that. It helped ground him and keep him in the moment. That was one of the reasons he tried to go every morning. Right now, as he looked out at the sea, he took a deep breath of fresh air and sent a thought to Spark.

Good morning, he thought down the bond. *Maybe it isn't morning where you are. Whatever time it is, I hope you're okay. I'm out surfing. I think you'd like how the sunrise looks on the sea. Nothing else to report. Tell the others I say hi. I miss all of you.*

This morning Billy wore his favourite blue and black wetsuit. He wished he were wearing his super-suit made of magical dragon fabric, but he and his friends had left their super-suits deep inside Dragon Mountain, in case they ever went back and needed them again.

Even in his wetsuit, the water of the Pacific Ocean was cold and biting this morning as he waded into the waves. It made him miss the warm and lemon-scented waters of the Forgotten Sea in the Dragon Realm. But still, he was glad he lived near the sea. Close enough that he could go by foot from his house early in the morning without needing to ask his parents for a ride or take the bus. Something had drawn him one day to this spot, the cove he had named Secret Cove. Not the most original name, he knew, but it was apt.

This morning, the water was calm, but he knew he wouldn't have to wait too long for a wave to come. He sat up on his surfboard, legs dangling on either side of it into the water, and gently bobbed up and down in the sea as he gazed out at the horizon. The rising sun spread its rays across the sky, and he heard the familiar cry of seagulls soaring above him as the wind sprayed salty seawater in his face.

In the distance, he thought he saw a series of dark waves crest and then disappear back under the water. He frowned. They didn't look like waves usually did.

A strange, unsettling sensation spread through his body, and he felt cold. As if the water surrounding his legs had suddenly dropped in temperature. He swallowed and brushed his hair out of his eyes, keeping his gaze on the horizon. He reached down the bond towards Spark, even though he knew she wouldn't hear him in time to be able to do anything.

Spark, something weird is happening.

The wave-like shapes rose up again, and this time he was sure they weren't waves. Was it a shark? A group of sharks? No, it was far too large to be a shark fin. A huge whale breaching? Whatever it was, he needed to get out of the water, and fast.

But before he could turn and swim back to shore, everything went quiet and the ocean itself seemed to still.

Then a huge spike emerged from the ocean, water sluicing off it. Another spike appeared behind it, and then an entire head burst out of the sea. Billy reared back on instinct, nearly falling off his surfboard, but he couldn't take his eyes off the creature.

Its head was enormous, dark turquoise and glistening in the light, with the dark grey spikes that he'd first seen going from the top of its head all the way down its thick neck and body. It kept rising like a huge snake unfurling itself and stretching for the sky. On its face, giant webbed flaps fanned out from its cheeks, almost like wings. Its eyes were round and huge, glowing a bright turquoise. And staring straight at Billy.

Billy knew with a sudden calm certainty that it was a dragon. Not like any dragon he'd ever encountered before, but a dragon all the same. On one level he knew he should be petrified, but his overwhelming emotion was stunned amazement. What was a dragon doing in the Human Realm?

Suddenly, the giant sea dragon unhinged its jaws, showing rows and rows of sharp teeth, each tooth bigger than Billy, and let out a mighty roar, louder and more ferocious than Billy had ever heard. As it roared, a bolt of true terror coursed through Billy.

He winced and covered his ears, but strangely the sound went over and around him, as if it was seeking a target. Billy looked up and, to his amazement, realized he could *see* the sound travelling through the air in a shimmering, trembling spiral, heading straight towards the cliffs on the beach behind him. He followed the trajectory and gasped as the blast of energy and sound hit the top of the cliff, knocking off chunks of it onto the empty beach below in a thundering crash.

It wasn't just *any* dragon that had made its way into the Human Realm. It was an aggressive, powerful one. Billy glanced back at it and saw that it was lowering itself into the water, eyes still on him, as if it was about to charge. It was still far from Billy, at least a football field away, but he knew how fast dragons were. It would catch him in moments. He knew he had to stay calm – if he panicked, he'd be done for. But he could feel his palms sweating and his heart pounding in his chest.

Where was a wave when he needed one?

He flipped around on his board, paddling as fast as he could away from the giant sea dragon and back towards the shore. His arms ached as he swam faster than he ever had, and he felt the telltale spark of energy run through him – the one that meant he was using whatever was left of his Lightning Pearl power of speed and agility.

He glanced back to see where the giant sea dragon was, and instead saw a cresting wave that rose up beneath him, propelling him forward back to shore. As he let the speed of the wave carry him, he glimpsed a dark-haired girl he'd never seen before standing knee-deep in the water and staring wide-eyed at the ocean behind him.

'Get out! Get out!' Billy shouted as he skidded past her on his board. 'Get out of the water now!'

She seemed to snap to her senses, shaking her head and turning and running out of the surf. Billy leaped up off his board and grabbed her hand, pulling her the rest of the way. Sand had never felt so good beneath his feet.

'It's . . . it's gone,' the girl said between gasps.

Billy looked back at the sea.

She was right. The giant sea dragon had disappeared without a trace.

Suspicious Secrets

'What *was* that thing?' Before Billy could respond, the dark-haired girl next to him kept talking. She had wide brown eyes, light brown skin and was wearing a bright orange wetsuit. 'I've been surfing since I was four and I've never seen anything in the ocean that looks like that. I thought you were a goner for sure.'

Billy didn't want to think about how close it must have been to him. He ran a hand through his hair and stared out at the sea, trying to glimpse a sign of the sea dragon. Because he knew that was what he had seen. Not that he was about to tell this girl that, especially when she had appeared on his secret beach uninvited.

'Maybe it was a shark,' he said, turning away from her and heading back up the beach.

'Do you think I have coconuts for brains? That *obviously* wasn't a shark,' the girl said, hands on hips. 'Have you ever seen a shark? Because I have. And let me tell you, that was no shark.'

Billy had actually never seen a shark in the ocean, only at the aquarium, and was begrudgingly impressed.

'What are you doing down here, anyway?' she went on. 'I never see anyone here.'

'I was about to ask you the same thing,' said Billy. 'This is kind of . . . my secret beach.'

The girl raised an eyebrow. '*Your* secret beach? Do you own it?'

Billy squirmed under her sharp gaze. 'Well . . . no. But I found it.'

'I didn't realize beaches fell under the "finders keepers" rule. Anyway, I found it too, so it's just as much my beach as it is yours. But I usually come in the afternoons, which must be why I've never seen you here before.'

Of course today of all days was when she had come early in the morning. Just Billy's luck.

'But, because I'm a kind and generous person, I'll share the beach with you,' the girl continued. Billy blinked, suddenly bewildered by how the conversation had turned. How had it gone from being *his* secret beach to her saying *she'd* share it with him? Before he could argue the point, the girl sighed dramatically. 'It isn't even that great a beach. You should see the beaches where I surf back home.'

'Home?'

'Hawaii.' She sighed longingly. 'We just moved here last month. I'm Lola, by the way. And before you ask, because everyone does, I'm hapa – Hawaiian and Chinese.'

Billy nodded in understanding. He was also used to people trying to figure out where he was from, even in California where there were plenty of people of mixed heritage like him. 'I'm Billy. And I get it – people ask me the same thing. I'm Chinese too, on my dad's side. And my mom's white. But more importantly, I don't think either of us should stick around on this beach for much longer. That . . .' Billy paused, 'thing might come back. And I think there was some sort of rockslide too.' He pointed behind Lola to where the pile of rocks and debris from the sea dragon's sound blast lay in a heap on the sand. 'Lucky you weren't standing there.'

Lola glanced over her shoulder and let out a yelp. 'No kidding!' Then she turned back to him, her dark eyes bright. 'So, what do we do now?'

'What do you mean?'

'Shouldn't we tell someone? A lifeguard? The coastguard? The news? Someone should know about that thing.'

'No!' Billy burst out. 'We can't tell anyone.'

Lola frowned. 'Why not?'

'Because ... because ...' Billy tried to think of a plausible excuse. The last thing he wanted was a news crew trying to find proof of a sea dragon. He needed to figure out what was happening, and to do that he needed time. And his friends.

And his dragons.

'Because?' Lola prompted.

'Because they won't believe us,' he said. 'They'll think we're kids playing a prank. Do you know how much trouble you can get into for lying to a lifeguard?'

'But we aren't lying.'

'They won't know that. Imagine if you hadn't seen . . . whatever that was. Would you believe it?'

Lola paused, and then blew a strand of hair out of her face. 'I guess you're right.' Then she grinned. 'But we should figure out what it is, don't you think? Do a stake-out! Get binoculars!'

Billy shook his head. 'No way,' he said. 'It's too dangerous. The best thing we can do is get out of here and forget we ever saw anything.' The last thing he needed was Lola snooping around.

Lola's grin faded to a puzzled frown. 'Why do I feel as if you're hiding something from me?'

Billy forced out a laugh. 'Don't be ridiculous. I just don't want us to get into any trouble, or get hurt. And who knows when that thing will be back. Or if there will be another rockslide. We should both stay far away from this beach.'

'You can do what you like,' said Lola. 'But I want to figure out what that was. This is the most exciting thing that has happened to me since I moved to California! Maybe the most exciting thing ever. Why are you so calm about this?' She scrutinized him again.

Right at that moment, Billy felt a fizz run through him, and then Spark's voice echoed in his head. *Billy? Are you all right? What happened?*

Hearing Spark's voice propelled Billy into action. He had to get home, he had to tell his friends what he'd seen and they had to get in contact with their dragons. If this girl wanted to stay on the beach and be eaten by a sea dragon, that was her problem. But even as he thought that, Billy knew he couldn't just leave her – for her own safety, as well as his fears that she might figure out more about the sea dragon than she should. He quickly sent a message back down the bond to Spark, wishing for the millionth time that they could communicate instantly like they could when they were near each other. *There's a dragon in the Human Realm. I'm fine, but something is wrong.*

Then he turned to Lola. 'I've got to get home. But let's meet up later. We can ... talk more about what we saw, okay? But not here. It's too dangerous here. I'll meet you for lunch tomorrow at Shakey's Café. Noon?'

'Tomorrow? Anything could happen by tomorrow!' Lola said.

This was exactly Billy's plan. By tomorrow, he hoped to somehow be back in the Dragon Realm. Or at least well on his way to figuring out what a sea dragon was doing in the Pacific Ocean.

'I've got ... plans today,' he said to Lola.

Lola put her hands on her hips again. 'Plans that are more important than solving the mystery of a giant sea monster?'

'Something like that,' he said. 'But I'll see you tomorrow. Now, come on, let's get off this beach. Unless you want to stay here by yourself?'

Lola looked at the pile of rubble, then at the sea, and sighed heavily. 'I guess you're right,' she said. 'I don't really want to face that thing alone.' She smiled at Billy. 'Good thing we both found this beach, huh?'

Billy nodded. He was strangely glad that someone else had witnessed the sea dragon, even if Lola didn't know what it was. Of course he wished that his friends, his real friends, had been with him for this, but at least he hadn't been alone.

As they walked towards the cliffs, something occurred to Billy. He turned to Lola with a smug expression. 'It might not be my beach, but to get

down here you've been using the ladder that I put up.'
He pointed at the makeshift ladder hanging against
the cliffs.

Lola laughed. 'Fine, the ladder belongs to you. But
I bet I would have figured out how to get down here
one way or another.'

Billy didn't doubt it. They made their way back
up the cliffs in silence, Billy's mind whirring with
possible explanations for why a sea dragon had been
in the Human Realm. He hoped it was going to stay
hidden, but he had a terrible feeling that this wasn't
the last he would see of the dragon.

Bacon, Eggs and Lying for Breakfast

By the time Billy got back home, his parents were up and had started to make breakfast. They were used to him leaving to surf hours before they woke up. And as long as *they* didn't have to wake up early to drive him to the beach, they didn't mind. But he had to be home in time for breakfast.

'Good morning,' said his dad cheerfully as he cracked an egg into a hot frying pan. 'How were the waves this morning?'

Billy's mind went blank. He didn't like lying to his parents more than he had to, and he was already keeping a pretty huge secret from them about what had happened this summer.

'The waves were . . . good,' he managed. 'Wave-like, you know.'

His mom raised an eyebrow over her cup of coffee. 'Wave-like?'

'Mmm-hmm. Big. Wet. Tubular. They were good. Not the best, but good.' He could hear himself rambling but couldn't stop. 'And I met someone new. A girl who moved here from Hawaii.'

'Oh, you met the Lam girl? Lola? I met her mom last week. I told you about her – don't you remember?' his mom said.

Billy restrained himself from rolling his eyes. His mom was the self-designated welcome brigade for anyone new in the neighbourhood. She was always telling him about new people who had moved in, and he usually wasn't paying attention.

'I'm glad you two met. You know she won the last regional surf championship in Hawaii?'

That caught Billy's attention. No wonder she'd been down at the beach on her own.

'Anyway,' Billy's mom went on, 'Lola and her mom are coming over for dinner tonight.' Billy nearly spat out his orange juice. *Tonight?* His mom continued talking, completely unaware of Billy's inner turmoil. 'I'm just trying to decide what to make. What do you think?'

'Er ... food?' Billy said. Oh no. This was terrible. How was he going to convince Lola not to say anything at dinner about what they'd seen? He had a sinking feeling that she wouldn't be able to keep it in. It was one thing asking her not to go to the news, and something else entirely asking her not to tell her own mom. Unless Lola also didn't want her mom to know she spent her time surfing at a remote beach with no lifeguard. He had to hope that was the case.

His dad slid a plate of eggs, bacon and toast in front of him. 'Did a wave knock the words out of you? Seems as if you're having some trouble forming sentences.'

Billy shook his head. 'Just tired. I swam out pretty far.'

'Not too far, I hope,' said his mom. 'The ocean can be unpredictable, you know.'

Oh, he knew.

'Don't worry,' he said, the lie tasting sour in his mouth. 'I'm always safe.'

*

After he finished breakfast, Billy hurried into his room and shut the door. He quickly looked at the clocks he had set up on his wall. Nine a.m. here in California, twelve p.m. in Atlanta, five p.m. in Ireland, and midnight in Ling-Fei's hometown in China. Hmm. What were the chances Ling-Fei was awake?

He quickly sent a message on the group chat. **Hey. Everyone around? We need to talk. Something weird happened today. Something ... like this-summer weird.**

They never texted details about what had happened. How would they explain if someone saw their messages? Dylan was especially paranoid that their phones would be hacked by secret government agencies and they'd be taken away for questioning. Billy wasn't sure if he believed that completely, but he didn't want to take any risks.

Ling-Fei responded first. **I'm awake!**

I was about to go out for lunch, but this sounds important, Charlotte chimed in. **Even more important than a pulled pork sandwich.** Even though Billy had just finished breakfast, his stomach growled at the thought of a pulled pork sandwich.

Dylan next. Give me a minute. I need to kick my sister out of my room. Dylan had four sisters, and from what Billy could tell, they were always in his hair.

A few minutes later his phone buzzed and a video screen popped up. And there were his friends. Despite everything that had happened that morning, he felt a rush of calm at seeing their faces. He wasn't alone. He had them. They'd faced bigger things than this and won. They could handle a rogue dragon appearing out of nowhere, right?

He didn't waste any time telling them what had happened.

'A SEA DRAGON?' Dylan shouted.

'For someone who's so worried about being overheard by the government, you sure do shout about dragons a lot,' said Charlotte. 'And how sure are you it was an actual dragon?'

'If Billy says it was a dragon, it must have been a dragon,' said Ling-Fei. She was wearing her pyjamas, which were appropriately covered in dragons.

'It definitely was a dragon,' Billy said firmly. 'But not like one we've ever seen before.'

'So . . . what do we do?' said Dylan. Then he paled.

'You aren't thinking of trying to track it down, are you? Just you and your surfboard and a giant evil-sounding sea dragon?'

Billy actually had considered it. 'Well . . .'

'Billy Chan! You'd better not,' ordered Charlotte. 'At least not until we can get there.'

'You know we'd never let you do something that dangerous on your own,' said Ling-Fei. 'We stick together, remember?'

'School starts in three weeks! I can't go gallivanting around the world chasing dragons!' Dylan burst out. 'Especially not evil dragons! We just did that!'

'Priorities, Dylan,' said Charlotte. 'If you need to miss a few days of school to save the world again, you can figure it out.'

'And what exactly am I meant to tell my parents?' Dylan said. 'Oh, just hopping on a plane to California to battle a dragon?'

'I don't think we'd meet here in California,' said Billy. 'I think we need to go back to the Dragon Realm. We need our dragons for this. Whatever's going on, I think it's big.'

Big enough that they couldn't face whatever was happening on their own.

When they'd said goodbye to their dragons at the end of their time at camp, the dragons had promised the friends could always find a way to them. The dragons' plan had been to bring peace back to the Dragon Realm, and also investigate to see if they could find any other portals between the Human and the Dragon Realms. So far they only knew about the one at Dragon Mountain, but they suspected there were more.

'What if we need you? And you're far from Dragon Mountain?' Billy had asked.

'Then I will create a portal,' Spark had replied, her gold antlers buzzing with power. 'Remember, Billy, the heart bond between a human and dragon cannot be broken. Not even across the realms.'

Billy knew that he couldn't ask Spark to use a considerable amount of power to open a portal between the realms just because he missed his dragon. But this was different. There had to be an open portal somewhere, because that sea dragon had come into the Human Realm.

'Oh, sure, because jumping into the Dragon Realm is even easier than getting to California,' said Dylan now, drawing Billy back to their present predicament.

'It actually might be,' said Ling-Fei thoughtfully. 'It's certainly faster.'

'And cheaper,' added Charlotte, who had already set up her own bank account. She said it was either to travel the world one day or to pay for university.

'And infinitely more dangerous!' sputtered Dylan. 'And crucially, none of us live near any portals.'

'That we know of,' said Billy. 'There must be one somewhere in the Pacific Ocean. How else would that sea dragon have come through into our realm?'

'I think you're forgetting a key thing about magical giant dragons.' Dylan's worried face pixilated for a moment on the screen. 'Dragons can move very fast, and they all have different powers. Maybe this one can teleport! We have literally no idea where that sea dragon came from. It could have hopped out of a volcano in Hawaii for all we know.'

'Hawaii is still in the Pacific Ocean,' Billy said peevishly.

'My point still stands,' Dylan went on. 'Where are we going to find portals?'

'We aren't going to find any portals,' said Ling-Fei serenely. 'We're going to ask the dragons to make them.'

Unexpected Dinner Guests

Billy knew from experience that creating portals was a tricky and unpredictable art. He'd only witnessed it on a handful of occasions. The first time he'd seen Spark create a portal, she'd had the power to do so because she'd swallowed a star. It turned out, while swallowing a star made dragons hugely powerful, it also awakened a craving in them for dark magic. A craving that Spark had been unable to resist, leading her down a path where she had done whatever it took to get her fill of dark power. It had nearly killed her. She'd died, Billy had seen it happen, and then she'd risen from the ashes as a new Spark. A Spark who had lost her taste for dark magic. A Spark Billy knew he could trust again.

And as much as Billy trusted her, it made him nervous thinking of her exerting so much power again. Even if it was for a good cause such as opening a portal to connect them. He just had to hope that Spark was powerful enough without the help of dark magic to open a portal. Because if Billy had learned anything, it was that doing bad things for a good reason didn't always work out the way you hoped.

But their dragons were powerful. And working together, maybe even with the help of other strong dragons, they would be able to open new portals.

And, of course, once a new portal was created, it came with a whole new set of problems. There was a reason that the portals between the Human and Dragon Realms were often hidden, and sometimes even protected by dragons.

The Dragon Realm was a dangerous place for humans. And the Human Realm was an equally dangerous place for dragons. While some dragons, like the ones heart-bonded to Billy and his friends, sided with humans and saw their value, not all dragons did.

Like humans, there were good dragons and some

who were not as good. And one of the worst things that could happen was for a dragon with a dark heart to find and bond with a human who had a heart equally as dark. That was exactly what had happened with the Dragon of Death and Old Gold.

Opening new portals came with a tremendous amount of risk.

But it was a risk Billy felt they had to take.

'Hey, guys,' said Charlotte suddenly, drawing Billy's attention back to their video call. 'I just remembered something. Did you see the news reports the other day about how the Crown Jewels have been mysteriously stolen in London? And someone claimed they saw a dragon do it? The person was laughed at but . . .'

'Oh, yeah,' said Dylan. 'That was weird.'

'I think it was more than weird,' said Charlotte. 'I wonder if it's connected.'

Ling-Fei gasped. 'That isn't the only strange report! In Beijing, someone, or *something*, broke into the Forbidden City in the middle of the night and stole the Eternal Territorial Integrity Gold Cup!'

There was a pause. 'And that is . . . ?' said Dylan.

Ling-Fei sighed. 'Of course you all know what the

British Crown Jewels are, but even after spending a summer in China you still don't know our treasures! It's one of the most important items in the Forbidden City.' She sighed again. 'It's a fancy gold cup. With jewels.'

'Ohhhh,' said Charlotte. 'I like the sound of that!'

'Do you think it was a dragon?' Ling-Fei went on.

'We do know how much they love shiny things,' said Dylan.

Billy frowned. 'I don't know. Do you guys really think dragons are behind this? The sea dragon I saw was huge. There is no way it could have sneaked into the Tower of London or Forbidden City without anyone seeing it.'

'Think about Xing,' said Ling-Fei. 'Don't you remember how fast she is? When she first took us into the mountain?'

It was a good point. Xing could move so fast that you barely saw her. She became nothing more than a silver blur, leaving only a gust of wind in her wake.

'Or Midnight,' Ling-Fei went on. Midnight wasn't heart-bonded to any of them – she was a young dragon they had met in Dragon City who had helped them. She had the power to cloak herself, and any others, in complete darkness.

'And I don't believe in coincidences,' said Charlotte, tossing her hair. 'Plus, like I said, somebody claimed they saw a dragon in London.'

'Why don't we try to contact our dragons and see what they think about all of this?' said Dylan. 'Billy?'

Billy was the only one who had the unique ability to speak to his dragon through his mind. He nodded. 'I've already tried to get in contact. But wherever Spark is right now, it's far from here. Sometimes I don't hear back from her for days.'

'At least you get to hear from her,' said Charlotte forlornly. 'I wish I could talk to Tank the way you can talk to Spark.'

'Same,' sighed Ling-Fei.

'What should I tell her?' Billy said.

'What you told us,' said Dylan. 'Big scary sea dragon in the Human Realm. Weird things happening.'

'And that, if they can, we need the dragons to figure out a way to get to us,' added Ling-Fei.

'This is the bit that gets a little murky for me,' said

Dylan. 'So let's just say, sure, the dragons can open portals to get to us. Is the plan for Buttons to burst into my kitchen? Say hello to my mum?'

Billy snorted at the image.

'We'll figure out the details later,' said Charlotte impatiently. 'First things first, Billy gets in touch with the dragons. We see if they can even get to us. We go from there.'

'Ah, I see, so we'll be winging it. Like the good old days,' said Dylan, but he was grinning. 'As long as we've got this all wrapped up by the time school starts. I'm really excited about taking my first chemistry class!'

'Of course you are,' said Billy with a laugh.

Billy felt buoyed by his chat with his friends. They had a plan. Or at least, they had the start of a plan. And that was better than nothing.

Then he remembered that he was going to have to face Lola at dinner and groaned. Maybe he could pretend to be sick? No, that would never work. He'd just have to hope that she would play it cool. And if she brought it up, well, he'd simply act as if he had no idea what she was talking about. He didn't feel good about it, but there was no other option.

Billy's parents prepared a feast for dinner. His dad had made his speciality: slow-cooked pork ribs in a spicy sauce, with garlic broccoli and a mountain of steamed rice. For dessert his mom baked her signature vanilla pound cake with freshly whipped cream and juicy strawberries. And Billy had been in charge of the appetizer. As it was his choice, he did one of his favourites: tortilla chips with guacamole and salsa. He'd been mashing avocados all afternoon.

Billy looked at the table full of food with a grin as he sneaked a chip into the guacamole. Sure, each course was a different type of cuisine, but it was all delicious. With any luck, Lola would be so busy eating all of the food that she wouldn't say a word.

By the time the doorbell rang, Billy had relaxed. He had everything completely under control.

Or so he thought.

When he opened the door, Lola bounded in with the same level of excitement Billy usually associated with a Labrador puppy.

'Isn't this amazing timing? I knew some new neighbours had invited us over for dinner, but I didn't realize it was you! We have *so much* to talk about!'

From behind her, a dark-haired woman wearing a bright purple dress laughed. Billy assumed she was Lola's mom. She looked like an older version of Lola, with the same light brown skin, wide smile and wavy dark hair.

'You must be Billy,' she said warmly, her dark eyes crinkling at the corners as she smiled. 'Aloha! I'm Lola's mom. You can call me Cynthia. Mrs Lam sounds far too old! And I see you already know Lola. I hear you're a surfer as well?'

Billy was so overwhelmed by the fact that Lola and her mom were here, at his house, and at any moment Lola could tell everyone what had happened at the beach that all he could do was nod.

'Wonderful,' Lola's mom went on. 'I still like to get out on the waves when I can. Lola's been surfing since she could walk!'

'Wow,' said Billy, and he meant it. 'I only started a few years ago.' As long as they kept the conversation on surfing, and only surfing, not mysterious, giant sea creatures appearing out of the depths of the ocean, they'd be fine.

'Come in, come in!' cried his mom, bustling everyone into the dining room. 'Billy made the guacamole and he's very excited for you both to try it.'

'Mom,' said Billy, flushing with embarrassment. 'It's just guacamole.'

'And it's delicious! Now what would everyone like to drink?'

As everyone got settled around the table, his parents chatting with Lola's mom about her job and how she was finding California, Lola kept shooting Billy meaningful looks. When it was clear nobody could hear her, she leaned over and whispered, 'I did some research.'

'Tell me about it tomorrow,' Billy said through clenched teeth.

'I think it was a dragon,' Lola went on. 'It looked kind of like a dragon, didn't it?'

'I didn't get a very good look at it,' Billy said, alarmed. 'Anyway, dragons aren't real.'

It pained Billy to say something like that, as if he was somehow betraying Spark and the others. But what else was he supposed to do?

'Rib?' he said, nudging the huge bowl of steaming ribs and sauce towards Lola, hoping to distract her.

Suddenly he felt a warm glow throughout. Spark! He hoped she hadn't somehow heard him say that dragons aren't real.

Her voice echoed inside his head, the clearest it had been since they'd been separated.

Billy, I am so glad you are safe. I do not know what a dragon is doing in your realm. I worry something is very wrong. We have found many new openings between the realms. Openings where there should not be any. It could be connected. I agree that we must reunite to figure out what is happening.

'Are you okay?' said Lola, staring at him. 'You're making a weird face.'

'I'm fine,' said Billy quickly. 'Er, just . . . really hungry.'

'Billy is always hungry,' said his dad with a laugh. For a moment Billy panicked that his dad had overheard what he and Lola had been talking about, but then his dad turned back to Lola's mom with a question about the air quality in Hawaii. Thank goodness adults were so easily distracted by the most boring conversation topics.

With a sigh of relief, Billy quickly spoke through his mind back to Spark. *Spark! I'm so glad you agree. What should I tell the others? Where should we meet you? And how?*

He knew it would take a while for her to reply. At least he couldn't worry too much while he waited. He picked up one of the ribs and gnawed on it, glad to see Lola and her mom were doing the same.

Spark's reply shot into his mind, surprising him so much that he nearly choked.

Billy, I hear you so much clearer now. I am glad for it, but it worries me because the veil between our worlds should not be so thin. We must move fast. I will try to open a portal on the beach where you saw the sea dragon. I have seen in your mind where it is. Meet me there at midnight.

Lola whacked him on the back. 'Don't worry,' she said. 'I'm a junior lifeguard!'

'I'm . . . fine,' Billy said between hacking coughs. A piece of chewed-up pork rib shot out of his mouth.

'There it is,' said Lola with satisfaction. She handed him his water.

'Sorry,' Billy said to the whole table. 'Went down the wrong pipe.'

Spark's voice echoed in his mind. *Billy? Is something wrong? Why are you not replying?*

'All fine. Just surprised,' he said out loud as he simultaneously thought it.

'Surprised by what?' said Lola.

'By how . . . delicious these ribs are. Your best ones yet, Dad!'

I do not blame you for being surprised. I must start to prepare the portal. I will see you at midnight. And reach out to me immediately if anything else strange happens.

The connection with Spark was so clear it was almost as if they were right next to each other. She was right, it was nice, but Billy knew it meant that something was very wrong. He managed to keep a smile on his face for the rest of dinner, even as his increasing worry made his stomach feel as if it was tied in knots, and every bite, no matter how delicious, was a struggle. Soon he'd be with Spark, he told himself, and she'd know what to do. Everything would be fine.

Explosion in the Sky

Billy thought dinner would never end.

Lola and her mom were there for hours and he had to force himself to stay at the table and act normal. When they finally left, with Lola giving Billy another meaningful look while saying, 'I'll see you tomorrow at Shakey's,' he couldn't close the door behind them fast enough.

Luckily, after that his parents went up to bed, and he was able to disappear into his room to prepare for meeting Spark at midnight. His mind was whirring with everything that had happened today. What was going on? Even after the adventure he'd had this summer, he had never expected dragons to come crashing into his world. How had a sea dragon even got into the Human Realm? Was Spark really going to create a portal between the Dragon Realm and his hometown? Billy's blood ran cold as the memory of what had happened the last time Spark created a portal twisted its way into his mind. The edges of the memory were still sharp enough to make Billy wince.

Billy shook the thought from his head. Spark was stronger now. Better. Billy could trust her. And as he thought it, he sensed the strength of their bond swell in his chest. Spark was getting closer – he could feel it. Ever since he had left Camp Dragon and their only entry point into the Dragon Realm, he had felt as if part of him was empty – as if he was an incomplete jigsaw, its missing pieces lost somewhere far away. And now some of those pieces were re-emerging, snapping back into place as if they had never been gone at all.

Spark, are you there? It's almost midnight here, but I haven't heard anything from you in hours. Is everything okay?

He waited for his dragon to respond. Nothing. He had been trying to get back in contact with Spark since dinner without any luck. It was odd that he could feel Spark getting closer, but he wasn't able to communicate with her. He guessed it was because Spark was so focused on creating the portal that she wasn't able to use their bond to speak with him.

Billy looked at the clock on his nightstand: 23:45. Time to go to the beach.

Billy sent a quick message to his friends. Going to try to meet up with Spark. Will message more soon.

He pocketed the phone and slipped out of his room, careful to avoid the loose board in front of his door. He remembered how angry his father had been when he and Eddie had shaken the floorboard loose during a game of tag, and how easily Eddie had calmed him down. The memory brought a smile to his face. When it came to convincing his parents to see things a certain way, no one had more skill than Eddie. He wished his brother were here with him now instead of taking a summer course at university. As much as he wanted to, Billy hadn't told his brother about the Dragon Realm or his adventures there. Or the fact that he had an unbreakable heart bond with a real, fire-breathing dragon. He'd thought about telling

Eddie about the dragons, but he'd agreed with his friends and their dragons that it was best they kept everything that had happened a secret. And even if he had decided to tell Eddie, he didn't know how he'd explain what had happened without it sounding ridiculous.

This was the first time Billy had ever sneaked out of his house, and it made him almost as nervous as the idea of Spark opening a portal into the Human Realm. He hoped that he'd be back home before his parents realized that he was gone, and that whatever was happening was something he and Spark could figure out right away. But just in case things took longer, he'd written a note that he left on the kitchen table:

Gone to a friend's house, back soon.

It wasn't a total lie. Spark was a friend, and the Dragon Realm was where she lived . . .

His parents were used to Billy leaving early in the morning to surf, so he knew it would be a while before they got really worried. Still, he felt a stab of guilt as he crept past their bedroom. But he steeled himself. This was too big and too important for him to panic about getting into trouble.

He made it outside, his heart pounding as he hurried down the street. The night was still, which was the opposite of how Billy felt as he stuck to the shadows, trying to keep his emotions in check. A full moon hung low on the horizon as if it were filled with secrets. Billy had a strange feeling that he was being watched as he turned onto the small dirt trail that led to cliffs overlooking the ocean. The trail had been cut by the local council last year to provide a path to see the breath-taking views, but Billy wasn't interested in that. No sooner had the trail been completed, Billy realized that there was a way to climb down to the bay below if you knew where to look. He veered off the main trail to the spot where he had built a makeshift ladder with a rope and some old lawn furniture that someone had carelessly dumped in the woods nearby. The trees above blocked the moonlight, and Billy struggled to see, but he had used this path so many times in the last month that he could do it with his eyes closed.

The ladder took him a short way down to a ledge that he then followed to the bay below.

Billy took a quick glance at his watch: 00:07. Was Spark already here? Was she waiting for him on the beach? Billy strained his eyes, trying to spot anything out of the ordinary – anything that might be a sign of Spark or the portal she was trying to create.

Spark, are you here? I'm on the beach. He waited.

Nothing. The beach was deserted. Disappointment washed over Billy. He hoped Spark was okay. Maybe she had just got her timing mixed up.

A branch snapped behind Billy and he whirled around to see what it was.

'Billy, is that you?' said a familiar voice, too high-pitched to be Spark.

'*Lola?* What are you doing here?'

Lola dashed away from the base of the cliff towards Billy. 'I should ask you the same thing! I know we just met, but I could tell at dinner that you weren't telling me everything you know about what we saw today. And I couldn't stop thinking about the creature. It kept me up, so I went to look out of the window to see if there was anything else strange going on and there you were sneaking in the shadows! Obviously I followed you.' Lola flipped her hair back over her shoulders. 'So, tell me, Billy with all the secrets, what are you doing on this beach in the middle of the night?'

Billy couldn't believe it. The *last* thing he needed was his new neighbour following his every footstep. Spark could show up at any minute now. He had to find a way to get Lola back home. 'That's none of your business,' he replied, with more force then he intended. He took a calming breath. All he had to do was convince her everything was fine and that she should go home. 'Actually, I couldn't sleep either . . . I thought coming back here would help calm me down. I know I said we shouldn't return, but I thought maybe if I saw the beach again, looking normal, I'd be able to go back to sleep.'

Lola's stance softened. 'That makes sense. But why do I still get the feeling you aren't telling me the whole truth? You barely looked at me at dinner!'

Because I'm not telling you the whole truth, Billy thought anxiously, the back of his neck getting hot. He didn't know what else to say. The more he thought about how to reply, the hotter his neck and back became. It felt as if he was standing under a heater. One that was really, really hot. Billy shifted uncomfortably as Lola's gaze grew more intense. 'I think—'

'BILLY, LOOK OUT!' Lola yelled, diving and tackling Billy into the sand.

As he fell backwards, he saw an explosion in the sky. Bolts of electricity shot out in every direction from a swirling, blue ring that appeared from nowhere. A shimmering blue creature with golden antlers *swooshed* out of it, its huge wings flapping so fast that the sand from the beach swirled up into little tornados.

The dragon's gold eyes stared down at Billy.

Spark! You made it! Maybe be a little more discreet next time? Billy said through their bond, but he was smiling from ear to ear.

Billy! It is so good to see you again.

Spark dived out of the sky towards Billy.

Lola screamed as she grabbed Billy's wrist and tugged him back towards the cliffs. Her eyes were so wide Billy could see the whites all around her pupils. 'It's another one! Quick, we have to run!'

Spark landed with a *thump* next to Billy.

'Billy, come on!' yelled Lola as she turned to run, half dragging Billy away.

'It's okay,' said Billy, pulling free and walking back to Spark. He rested his hand on Spark's hind leg. 'I know this one.'

Lola turned back and froze, her mouth dropping open.

There was no getting out of this now. 'This . . . is a friend of mine. Her name is Spark.' Billy turned to Spark. 'And this is Lola.'

Lola scrambled backwards. 'I don't care what its name is. I care that it doesn't eat me!'

'Do not worry,' said Spark. 'I will not eat you. You are a friend of Billy, which means you are a friend of mine.' She bowed her head in greeting.

Lola's eyes shone with wonder, her fear quickly turning to awe. She stared at Spark, her mouth still half-open. 'A dragon!' she breathed. And then she turned to Billy. 'I knew that thing we saw was a dragon! You lied to me!'

Billy shrugged. 'You can't blame me.' He turned and gave Spark's enormous leg as much of a hug as he could manage.

Spark lowered her head and nuzzled Billy's shoulder. *I have missed you too, Billy.*

Billy looked up at Spark. 'I'm so glad you're here. I was worried something might have happened.'

'I am fine,' said Spark. 'But something strange is happening. The separation between the Dragon Realm and the Human Realm is thinner than it has ever been. It took far less effort to create the portal than I expected. It is why I punched through the portal so forcefully and made such a ... grand entrance.' Spark looked inquisitively at Lola. 'I am sorry if I startled you.'

Lola stared at Spark for a moment, still taking in what she was seeing. Then she grinned. 'I'll forgive you if you tell me what's going on.' She shook her head in amazement. 'This is so awesome.'

Spark let out a low chuckle. 'I like your new friend, Billy.'

She's not my friend, Billy said through their bond. *I just met her today. She's been following me everywhere.* Part of him was pleased that Lola was handling meeting a real life dragon so well, and part of him was annoyed she was already so comfortable with Spark. Spark was *his* dragon, after all.

Billy took a step towards Lola. 'Listen, I know you must have a lot of questions. I know I did when I first met Spark. You were right – we did see a dragon earlier today. Lots of dragons exist in a place called the Dragon Realm. But they shouldn't be showing up here. Something bad is happening and I have to go with Spark to figure it out. I think it's best if—'

'Oh, no, you don't, Billy Chan,' said Lola, cutting Billy off. 'If you think I'm missing out on this, you're out of your mind. Wherever it is you're going and whatever it is you're doing, I'm coming with you.'

Billy ran his hand through his hair and let out an exasperated breath before looking back up at Lola. 'It's too dangerous. You should go back home and forget this ever happened.'

'Forget this ever happened?' Lola said, pointing to the sky. 'There is an *enormous* electric portal swirling above our heads! I'm pretty sure the whole neighbourhood is about to come to this beach to see what's going on.'

'Lola is right,' said Spark. 'We must move quickly. I have left this portal open as creating a new one might make take more time than we have, and it might also be a bit more . . . explosive than would be acceptable. But it will not be long until others come to investigate. And Tank, Xing and Buttons are waiting for us on the other side.'

'What about Charlotte, Dylan and Ling-Fei? We need them too,' said Billy.

'Yes. I was able to find you because our bond is so strong. Now that we are together, you can help me repoint this portal to each of their locations using your connection with them.'

Billy raised an eyebrow. 'I don't have a heart bond with the others. You know that.'

'It does not have to be a heart bond, Billy,' replied Spark. 'You and your friends share a deep connection that you cannot see, but it is as real as true north is to a compass. And with you as my compass, we can bring everyone together again.'

Billy nodded, then he looked over at Lola. He knew that either she was coming with them, or she was going to tell *everyone* about what she had seen. The strange thing was, he found himself hoping she'd join him for the adventure. He held a hand out to Lola. 'Are you coming? It's now or never.'

'You bet I'm coming,' said Lola, grabbing Billy's hand. 'I wouldn't miss this for anything!'

Billy smiled and helped Lola climb onto Spark's back, and then he hopped on behind her. 'Hold on,' he said. Lola let out a squeal of delight. 'This is the most terrifying and amazing thing I've *ever* done. And I've jumped off cliffs *and* swum with sharks.'

'I am flattered,' said Spark. 'So, Billy, where to first?'

'Let's go and get Charlotte,' said Billy as Spark shot into the portal, the two children on her back. Billy glanced over his shoulder just in time to see moonlight shimmering on the ocean below, then the portal snapped shut and he couldn't see anything at all.

Portal Jumping

It had been a while since Billy had travelled through a portal, but he recognized the familiar feeling of being shot through a straw.

'This is amazing!' Lola cried as they zipped through the portal. Only a few moments passed before they burst out into another night sky. The air was thicker here, hot and humid. They were on a tree-lined residential street and directly in front of them stood a large brick house with a red front door and blue window shutters.

'Where are we?' asked Lola.

'This must be Charlotte's house in Atlanta,' said Billy, feeling distinctly exposed in the open air. 'It's three a.m. here, so hopefully everyone on this street is sleeping.'

Lola shot Billy an intrigued look. 'I mean, imagine what we would say if someone saw us ... "Don't mind us, stranger, we're just two regular kids riding a dragon in the middle of the night."'

Billy grinned. If Lola felt anxious about riding a dragon and travelling through a magical portal that teleported them across the country, she didn't show it. He remembered the first time he had ridden Spark – the joy and excitement that had flooded through him when she'd lifted up into the air with him on her back. It was a moment he would never forget, no matter how many times he flew with her.

'Well, let's not stay long enough for that to happen,' said Billy. 'We're going to find Charlotte and get out of here.'

Even though Billy had ridden Spark hundreds of times before, it felt completely different having Spark with him in the Human Realm. More real. More dangerous.

Billy grabbed his phone out of his pocket to text Charlotte. But the screen was blank and his phone wouldn't turn on. 'I don't think my phone survived the portal-jump,' he said, feeling silly. But what were they going to do now? He couldn't exactly ring Charlotte's doorbell in the middle of the night. He slid his phone back into his pocket and studied the house, trying to work out which room was Charlotte's. He remembered seeing a lamp post outside Charlotte's window in their video calls.

'Spark, take us over to the top right window. I've got a feeling that's Charlotte's room.'

Spark glided over to the house, careful not to knock over any trees, and hovered above the roof. 'This is as close as I can get without damaging anything,' Spark said in a hushed tone. She craned her neck down until her head was right in front of the window.

Billy darted up Spark's back and slid down her neck in two fluid motions.

'Wow,' whispered Lola. 'You move like a cat.'

Billy flashed her a smile as he hung from one of Spark's golden antlers. He felt more agile now that Spark was closer. 'There are some benefits to being heart-bonded with a dragon.'

'What does that mean?' said Lola eagerly. 'Can I be heart-bonded to a dragon too?'

'It's complicated,' said Billy. 'Spark is my heart-bonded dragon, and only mine.' His voice was filled with pride. 'If a dragon and a human have the same kind of heart, they can share a heart bond. It's a connection between you and the dragon. But it's super rare.'

Lola raised an eyebrow. 'Rarer than finding a dragon?'

'Even rarer than that,' said Billy. 'I'll tell you more about it later. Let's focus on getting out of here without terrifying the entire neighbourhood.'

The window shutters were open but the curtains inside were drawn. Billy cursed under his breath. He *really* hoped this was Charlotte's room. Billy reached out, gripped the window and pulled gently upwards. With a sharp *click* the window popped open.

He whispered as loudly as he dared. 'Charlotte. Charlotte. Are you in there? It's me. Billy.'

Billy held his breath, waiting for a response from behind the curtain. Still nothing.

He thought about how ridiculous they must look:

Spark, an enormous, electric-blue dragon hovering above the house, Billy dangling from one of her antlers. The thought gave him courage. They had to move *fast*, before anyone discovered them. He reached a hand through the opening in the window and slowly pulled the curtain to one side. To his amazement, he saw a bewildered Charlotte standing right in front of him, in hot-pink pyjamas, with a glittery eye mask on top of her forehead. Her eyes were wide with panic. Behind her, Billy could see her dad and stepmom sleeping in their bed. Whoops. He *had* picked the wrong room.

Charlotte held up a finger to her mouth with one hand and waved frantically for them to go away with the other. Spark swiftly pulled her neck back up and out of view of the window. A minute later, Billy saw Charlotte sneak out of the back door. She'd thrown a fuzzy, white sweater on over the top of her pyjamas.

'There she is!' said Billy.

Spark swooped down towards Charlotte, who jumped up onto Spark's back as soon as she'd landed.

'I was hoping I'd see you!' she said. 'After I got your text, I couldn't sleep. And then when you never replied to any of us . . . well, we figured something must have happened. I bet the others are waiting for you too.' Then she grinned and shook her head. 'Y'all are lucky my dad and stepmom are such deep sleepers!'

She paused and eyed Lola. 'And who is *this*?'

'A new friend,' Billy said quickly. 'No time to explain. We need to get out of here before anyone sees us. You ready?'

Charlotte nodded. 'I'm always ready.'

Billy glanced at her phone. 'That won't work after we portal-jump, so before we go, can you text the others to tell them we're on our way?'

Charlotte nodded and quickly typed into her phone. Then she paused. 'I guess I should text my parents something too, huh?' Billy nodded, and Charlotte went back to her phone for a moment before putting it in her pocket.

'Even if it's going to get fried in the portal, I don't want to risk anyone reading my messages,' she said.

'Smart,' said Billy admirably. Then he turned to Spark. 'All right, Spark, let's go to Ireland next and pick up Dylan.'

Without another word, Spark shot up into the sky and back through the open portal.

Billy felt the squeeze of being pushed through the portal again, except this time, as they neared the exit, he could tell that something was off. Spark was backpedalling, trying to stop, and yet they were still hurtling forward. It was as if they were a speeding car on an ice-covered road.

'HOLD ON,' said Spark. 'BRACE YOURSELVES.' Spark curled her tail around Charlotte and Lola, pinning them close to her body. Then they crashed out of the other side of the portal.

Billy held on tight as they smashed through what he thought was the inside of a house. Wood splinters exploded in all directions. If it wasn't for their bond, which kept Billy glued to Spark like a magnet when they flew, he would have flown straight off Spark's back. And the only reason Charlotte and Lola were okay was because Spark's tail had held them in place.

'Is everyone all right?' said Spark, gently uncurling her tail from around Charlotte and Lola.

It took Billy a few seconds to figure out what had

happened. He blinked, letting his eyes adjust to the light all around him.

'That was bananas,' said Charlotte.

'I think I'm okay,' said Lola, sounding shaken.

'The portal acted in an extraordinarily unnatural way. It must have something to do with the strange things that are happening between the realms.'

'GUYS!' shouted a voice from below. 'WHAT ARE YOU DOING IN MY BATHROOM?'

Billy looked down and saw a soaking wet Dylan holding a shower curtain around himself. He was standing in what had previously been a bathroom in his house, but was now missing a roof and an exterior wall as if a tornado had torn it off, after the group had blasted through the portal. Thankfully, the rest of his house was still intact.

'Didn't you see Charlotte's text?' Billy said.

'No, because as you may have noticed, I WAS IN THE SHOWER. And then you blasted a hole in my bathroom!'

'My sincerest apologies, Dylan,' said Spark. 'Are you unharmed?'

Dylan patted himself down and examined his

limbs. 'Yeah, I think so.' He looked up at the hole in his roof. 'I'm not so sure about my house though.' He shook his head. 'Good thing my parents are out shopping with my sisters. I don't know how I'd explain this.'

Then he spotted Lola. 'Um ... who are you?'

'Oh, this is Lola. She's my neighbour,' said Billy.

'Well, why is she here?' said Dylan. 'No offence, but I wasn't expecting to make a new friend wearing nothing but a towel after a dragon crashed into my bathroom.'

'I'm here because clearly you guys need some backup,' said Lola. 'And I have an idea to help fix this. Why don't you have Spark put a tree against the house so it looks as if the wind blew the tree into the roof?'

'That's actually a really good idea,' said Charlotte. 'Usually I'm the one who comes up with all the great ideas, but I like that one a lot.'

Lola grinned. 'It's because that once happened to my grandma's house. There was this huge hurricane in Hawaii and a tree went through her kitchen!'

'I hope your grandmother was unharmed,' said Spark.

'Oh, she was fine! She was just mad that the tree broke her favourite tea set,' said Lola.

'It's a good idea,' Billy agreed.

Dylan frowned as he looked up at the very blue sky through the hole in his roof. 'I guess there could have been a storm just over my house that nobody else saw?'

'Unless you have a better idea?' said Billy. 'Also, you should put some clothes on. And probably leave your parents a note saying you saw the wind knock the tree over!'

'A note,' Dylan repeated.

'Better than nothing,' said Billy.

Dylan sighed deeply. 'I'm going to be grounded for ever.'

While Dylan got dressed and left a hastily written note for his parents explaining that the wind had knocked a tree over onto the roof, and he'd gone to a friend's house for the afternoon in case the roof caved in any more, Spark pulled up a tree and leaned it against the house to back up Dylan's story. Then she hid in the garage before any neighbours spotted her. The portal was still swirling above Dylan's house, but there was nothing they could do about that. All they could hope for was that anyone passing by would think it was a strange cloud.

When the four children went into the garage, Spark was inspecting a car with great interest. 'I have never seen a human car up close,' she said as Billy and the others came in. 'How does it turn on?'

'With a key. I'll show you another time,' said Billy. Then something occurred to him. He turned to Dylan. 'Do you have your phone?' Dylan nodded. 'One, text Ling-Fei and tell her to meet us by the mountain. Two, you should leave your phone here. Portal-jumping fries them.'

'Dragon Mountain?' asked Dylan as he started to text on his phone.

'Where else?'

Return to the Dragon Realm

The journey from Dylan's house in Ireland through the portal and back to Dragon Mountain took mere moments. The portal itself opened deep inside the mountain, right on top of a gigantic mound of jewels.

Charlotte laughed as she stepped out of a pile of rubies. 'I see we've landed in Xing's hoard!' Xing was Ling-Fei's dragon, and she collected precious jewels and gems. 'Our super-suits should be here somewhere . . .' She looked around the cavern, trying to see where they'd left them. Her eyes lit up. 'Ah-ha! Here they are.'

'And Ling-Fei should be here soon,' said Dylan. 'I hope she got my text.'

'I was already here!' called out a voice in the dark. Everyone looked towards the sound, and Ling-Fei emerged, her smile even brighter than the flashlight she carried.

'How did you know?' said Billy with a wide grin.

'Well, when you said you were going to meet Spark on the beach near your house, I figured it was only a matter of time before we met up back here. Where else would we meet before going on another adventure?'

Charlotte dashed forward and pulled Ling-Fei into a huge hug. 'You, my friend, are brilliant.'

Ling-Fei hugged her back, and then her eyes landed on Lola. 'I'm guessing you came with these guys? Or have you been hiding in here?'

Lola grinned and waved. 'I'm Billy's new neighbour. I kind of got sucked into all of this by accident. My name's Lola.'

'If by that you mean you insisted on coming along,' said Billy, but he was grinning. It felt good to be back in Dragon Mountain, and to be back with his friends.

There was a sudden blur of silver, and Xing appeared. 'Hello, human children. I thought I heard you in here chit-chatting. Put on your suits and then come quickly. We are waiting for you on the other side of the mountain.'

Outside the mountain, on the Dragon Realm side, Tank and Buttons stood silhouetted against the inky sky. Billy remembered that time worked slightly differently in the Dragon Realm, and he wondered what time it was back at home. Had his parents realized he was gone by now?

But before he could dwell too much on it, Buttons bustled over with a wide, toothy smile. 'Where is my human?' he said. 'Dylan, my boy!' He held out his arms for a hug, like a doting auntie, and with a laugh, Dylan embraced his dragon.

'Hello, Buttons,' he said. Then he reached into his pocket. 'I brought you something.' He held out a handful of brightly coloured buttons.

'My favourite!' said Buttons, beaming.

'Sorry I didn't bring you a present,' Billy said to Spark.

'That is fine,' she said. 'Seeing you again is the best gift there is.' Billy felt his cheeks flush at his dragon's praise.

'Tank!' cried Charlotte, catapulting herself towards

her giant dragon. 'I've missed you so much!' Tank scooped her up in his enormous claws and lifted her up so they were eye to eye.

'I have missed you too,' he said.

'Whoa,' said Lola, tilting her head back to take Tank in.

'It is good to see you all again,' Tank said solemnly. 'Even under the circumstances.'

Tank looked even bigger than Billy had remembered. He guessed that when they'd been with their dragons every day, they had grown used to their size and their magnificence. He'd almost forgotten how incredible, how imposing, they were.

He saw his wonder reflected and magnified in Lola's face. If she was frightened, she was doing a good job of hiding it. She stared at each of the dragons in turn, eyes wide in amazement. 'So this is why you stayed so calm when that sea dragon chased you. You're used to giant dragons!'

'The sea dragon *chased* you?' burst out Dylan. 'You kept that key detail quiet.'

'It was chasing . . . something. I don't know if it was me,' said Billy.

'Well, we need to find out what that dragon was doing in the Human Realm, and what it was chasing,' said Ling-Fei. She reached up and stroked Xing's head. 'Xing, you're looking especially sparkly, you know. I think I forgot just how beautiful you are!' Xing preened. Ling-Fei gazed at the rest of the group. 'You all look wonderful! I've missed all of you so much!'

Dylan cleared his throat. 'I've missed everyone too, but I'll admit I'd rather us be meeting up for a fun get-together, not because there's a rampant dragon on the loose.'

'I fear the mysterious sea dragon is only the beginning of our problems,' said Spark. 'Strange things are happening in our realm. Things that should not be happening. It seems to have started in the past few days, but it looks as if it is escalating.'

'Is it the Dragon of Death?' Even just saying her name gave Billy goosebumps. 'Is she back?'

Buttons shook his head. 'Not that we know of.'

'She won't be coming back, not ever,' said Xing.

'You thought that before though, didn't you?' said Charlotte.

'That was different.' Xing's voice was sharp. 'We

learned from our mistake. Before we had merely sent her back in time. Now she is forever banished into a black hole in the furthest reaches of outer space. Not even light can touch where she is.'

Lola rubbed her eyes. 'The Dragon of Death? Going back in time? Outer space? What the heck are you all talking about?'

'It's kind of a long story,' Ling-Fei said kindly. 'But it's a good one!'

'You'll see that as soon as you accept the existence of real life, magical dragons, it's easy to believe anything else that's thrown at you,' added Dylan.

'Well, I definitely believe in the huge dragons standing right in front of me,' said Lola. Then she grinned. 'Unless I'm dreaming. And if I am, this is the coolest dream I've ever had!' She turned her attention from the dragons to the wide expanse all around them. 'And where exactly are we now?'

Billy had been so focused on the fact that they were all together again, and that the portals had worked, he hadn't actually noticed where they were.

They stood at the edge of Dragon Mountain, back where their adventure had begun, but on the

Dragon Realm side. He remembered what it had been like when he'd first seen it. Awe-inspiring, but desolate. The realm had been ravaged by nox-wings, the followers of the Dragon of Death who used dark magic to drain life force from the very earth itself, as well as from other living creatures.

Now, with dark magic banned, the land was thriving again. Even in the darkness, Billy could see lush plant life growing all around them. The sky was a deep indigo, and the three moons of the realm shone brightly amidst thousands of twinkling stars. Below the stars and the moons were the incredible floating islands. Some islands had waterfalls that flowed off them, crystal clear water rushing all the way to the ground below, and others were draped in thick foliage.

Most recognizable of all were the many peach trees that dotted the landscape. Even when the Dragon Realm had been poisoned by nox-wings, the peach trees had been there. The dragons claimed they were indestructible.

And that was because the peach trees weren't normal peach trees. Each peach tree had the potential to grow peaches of immortality. Take one bite, and become immortal. Of course it was incredibly rare to find a peach of immortality, but there was still a chance. Dylan had been so excited by this prospect he had eaten as many as he could when they'd first visited this realm. The only issue was there was no sure-fire way to test if you'd eaten a peach of immortality or a normal peach. The only living creature that Billy knew for sure had eaten a peach of immortality was a tiny gold flying pig that had saved them on more than one occasion.

Which reminded Billy. Where *was* Goldie? When he'd last seen the pig, he'd left it with the dragons.

'This is the Dragon Realm,' he said to Lola. 'It's where all dragons live, and all kinds of other creatures.' He turned to the dragons. 'I realize this might not be the most urgent question, but where is Goldie?'

'Goldie?' said Tank with a frown. Tank usually looked as if he was frowning – it was his default expression – but when he was perplexed, his giant brow furrowed rather comically. Not that Billy would ever tell Tank that.

Xing sighed. 'The pig. They've named it.'

'Well, we named all of you,' said Dylan.

'We are *dragons*. Of course you named us! That is part of the dragon–human heart bond. There is no reason to name a pig,' said Xing.

'Even one as cute as Goldie,' said Buttons.

'Oh, not you too,' said Xing with a groan.

'The pig is safe,' said Spark.

'It is always safe; it is *immortal*,' muttered Xing.

'The pig enjoys the company of the young dragon,' Spark went on. 'The one you call Midnight.'

Billy felt a rush of affection for the young dragon whom they'd met in Dragon City. Without her help, and the help of her family, who called themselves the Thunder Clan, Billy knew he wouldn't have survived the treacherous, futuristic city that had been run by the Dragon of Death herself.

Lola exhaled loudly and rubbed her temples. 'I'm trying to keep up, I really am, but this is a *lot* to take in.'

'At least you've got us to explain it to you,' said Charlotte. 'When we first met the dragons, they tried to eat us.'

'We most certainly did not!' sputtered Buttons.

'Well, you acted as if you wanted to eat us,' said Dylan.

'They had to!' Ling-Fei was unfailingly loyal. 'They had to test our bravery, remember?'

'Yes, yes. Loyal, strong, brave and true,' said Charlotte. 'We had to prove we were all four.' She turned back to Lola. 'I wonder which you are.'

'I'm all four, obviously.'

Charlotte stared at Lola for a beat, and then her face split into a wide grin. 'I like her,' she declared. 'She can stay.'

'That's good, because I don't think she was planning on going anywhere,' said Billy.

Lola grinned back at all of them. 'Let me see if I've got everything so far. You four somehow came into this realm, found these dragons, and then working together you all defeated this super-bad dragon called the Dragon of Death. And there are portals between our world and this one. But more are opening where they shouldn't be. Which is why we saw that sea-monster dragon at the beach. And nobody knows what's causing the portals to open, or who is doing it. Is that right?'

'Basically,' said Billy.

Dylan gave a slow clap. 'I'm with Charlotte – this one can stay. I don't even know if I could have summed it up that well, and I lived through it!'

Suddenly, the ground beneath them began to shake and roll.

'Quick! Children! On our backs!' cried Spark. Billy felt a familiar rush of adrenaline and fear as he grabbed Lola's hand and pulled her up with him onto Spark's back. Charlotte, Dylan and Ling-Fei all leaped up on their respective dragons. The dragons rose into the air, moving close together in a protective circle.

'Is it an earthquake?' said Billy, watching the ground beneath him undulate as if it were a stormy sea.

'We are not sure,' said Spark. 'It has been happening more and more.'

'And that isn't the strangest bit,' said Buttons gravely. 'Look to the left, at the distant mountains.'

Billy and the others followed his instruction. Even from a distance, Billy could see the mountains shaking.

Shaking so hard they were beginning to blur.

'That . . . that doesn't look right,' he said.

'Keep watching,' said Spark.

The mountains grew more and more blurry, as if Billy were staring at them through a pair of binoculars that he couldn't get into focus.

And then, with a *pop*, they disappeared completely.

Mysterious Disappearances

'WHERE DID THOSE MOUNTAINS GO?'

Dylan's shout echoed all around them. Usually, Billy thought Dylan had a tendency to overreact, but in this case he completely understood why his friend was panicking.

'We do not know,' said Spark.

'At first, we thought they were moving mountains. You know these things are possible here in our realm,' said Buttons.

Billy nodded. Once, when they'd needed to cross a great distance in this realm and didn't have their dragons, Ling-Fei had convinced a mountain to stand up and carry them to where they'd needed to go.

'And then we thought that perhaps a powerful dragon was making them invisible. You also know this is possible,' said Xing.

Again, Billy nodded. He'd seen Xing herself do it, casting a protective ring of reflection spell around them so they wouldn't be seen. And not only Xing. Midnight had the power to cloak herself, and any others, in complete darkness.

'Let me guess,' said Charlotte with a drawl. 'It isn't either of those things.'

'No. It is not,' said Tank. 'It is something we have never seen before. Something we do not understand.'

Ling-Fei shuddered. 'Whatever it is, it feels unnatural. Something is very wrong. It's off balance.' Ling-Fei had the gift of being able to connect to nature and magic and living things, a sense she shared with Xing.

'Is it a . . . portal? A portal gone wrong?' asked Billy, still staring at the place where the mountains had just stood.

'It is not like any portal we have ever encountered before,' said Spark. 'We have stayed far from the areas where we have seen it happening as we do not want to risk being taken along with the landscape. But it is happening more and more. Sometimes it is a single tree, and other times it is as you just witnessed. Sightings started several days ago, but each day more things are disappearing. Valleys. Mountains. Entire lakes.'

'We have witnessed some dragons fall into these spots as well. And they have not been seen again,' added Tank gravely.

'So what you're saying,' said Dylan, 'is that dragons *and* entire chunks of the Dragon Realm itself are disappearing.' He let out a low whistle. 'Cool. Cool. Cool. That isn't absolutely terrifying or anything at all.'

Buttons laughed gently. 'It's not as dire as it seems. We're hopeful that they're reappearing somewhere else. If these soft spots, as we call them, indeed are a type of portal.'

'What if . . .' Billy spoke slowly, the thought taking shape like water turning into ice. 'What if that sea dragon I saw came through one of those soft spots? What if they *are* portals between our realms?'

'You know I don't believe in coincidences, but

wouldn't someone notice if dragons started appearing in the Human Realm? Or entire mountain ranges!' said Charlotte sceptically.

'Didn't a lake appear in the middle of the English countryside a few days ago?' said Lola suddenly. 'On a sheep farm. I saw it on the news. The farmer claimed it had appeared overnight, and his neighbours laughed and said it must have been a flood. But I saw the footage – it was an entire lake.'

Dylan scratched his head. 'You know what?' he said. 'My cousin Maeve told me about a woman outside Dublin who was sure her land had turned into a kind of miniature desert. Sand everywhere. Global warming was the official reason, but what if it really was a desert? What if it was a piece of desert from the Dragon Realm?'

'It does make a strange sort of sense,' said Ling-Fei.

'But who's opening the portals?' said Billy. 'And why?'

'There have always been doorways between our realms. This mountain being one of them,' said Xing. 'But whatever these are, they are not natural doorways. We did not know of these mysterious occurrences happening in your world. All we knew was that Billy saw a sea dragon.'

The five children and the dragons turned their attention back to the fuzzy area where the mountains had stood moments ago.

'We should stay far from there,' said Tank uneasily.

'It seems things are more complicated than we first thought,' said Spark.

'Aren't they always?' muttered Dylan.

'I'm glad we're together,' said Buttons. 'This is something we can all work to fix. For the good of both our realms.'

'I'm all for fixing things, but how can we fix something when we don't even know what the problem is?' said Charlotte. 'We don't have enough information.'

'Charlotte's right,' said Billy. 'We need to know more before we can do anything.'

Dylan raised an eyebrow. 'You want to *think* before you act? Who are you and what have you done with my best friend Billy?'

'Ha ha ha,' said Billy, rolling his eyes. 'Sometimes I can be sensible, you know.'

'So, what's the plan then?' said Lola eagerly. 'And when do I get my own dragon? You're all clearly paired up, so my dragon is coming soon, right?'

Xing let out a sharp laugh. 'It is not that easy, but I admire your attitude.'

'Heart-bonding with a dragon is a big deal,' Charlotte said to Lola. 'It doesn't just ... happen when you see a dragon for the first time.'

'Although that is what happened to us,' mused Dylan.

'I'm sure your dragon is somewhere,' Ling-Fei said with a smile. 'We'll find them.'

'Later,' interrupted Billy. 'We'll find them later. Right now we have bigger problems to deal with.'

Lola scowled at him. 'How am I supposed to help you all save the world – both worlds – if I don't even get my own dragon?'

'Your job is to make sure you stay alive,' said Billy. 'We'll handle the rest. We're practically professional world-savers now.'

Lola's scowl deepened. 'Are you always this annoying?'

'Yes,' said Dylan quickly. Then he grinned at Billy. 'You know what I mean.'

'You should consider yourself lucky to even be here,' said Charlotte to Lola. 'How many kids get to come into a magical Dragon Realm?'

'I mean … that guy is here,' said Lola, pointing over Charlotte's shoulder.

'What guy?' Billy whipped his head around. Was it JJ? JJ was their sometimes friend, sometimes foe, who had come through for them when it'd really mattered. After siding with the Dragon of Death, JJ and his dragon, Da Huo, had unexpectedly joined forces with Billy and the others to help defeat the Dragon of Death in Dragon City. Billy had wondered how JJ had been doing back home in China, and if he'd ever come into the Dragon Realm to see his dragon. Should they have sought him out too?

Before Billy could think any more about JJ, his gaze locked onto the person Lola was pointing at.

The person who was definitely not JJ.

Someone else was in the Dragon Realm.

Someone they didn't know.

The Lost Boy

The dragons were immediately on alert.

'Do any of you know that boy?' said Spark. 'Has he followed you in here?'

Because it was clear now that it was a boy – a boy who looked to be around their age. He had dark brown skin, short black hair and was wearing a bright red shirt.

Billy squinted. Was he in a soccer jersey?

The boy was wandering aimlessly, clearly lost, but then he stopped suddenly, as if he knew they were talking about him.

'I've never seen that boy in my life,' said Charlotte.

'Me neither,' added Dylan.

'Same,' said Billy, feeling completely bewildered. Who was this boy and how had he found his way into the Dragon Realm?

'Whoever he is, he looks lost,' said Ling-Fei.

'Only one way to figure out who he is and what he is doing here,' said Xing. 'Ling-Fei, hold on.' Moving so fast she turned into a blur of silver and scales, Xing raced through the air towards the boy, scooping him up with her tail so quickly that Billy would have missed it if he'd blinked.

'Ah, the old grab and fly,' said Dylan approvingly. He glanced at Lola. 'That's how we were first acquainted with Xing. She scooped us up and took us into the mountain. I thought we were goners for sure!'

Xing was already back, and she unceremoniously dumped the boy in the middle of them.

'Do not move,' she hissed warningly. The boy's brown eyes widened and Billy felt a pang of pity for him. He'd forgotten how terrifying the dragons were if you didn't know them.

Billy slid off Spark and landed easily in a crouch next to the boy. 'We don't mean to scare you,' he said.

'We just want to know who you are and what you're doing here.'

The boy seemed to take a moment to steel himself and then he looked directly at Billy. 'I'm Jordan Edwards,' he said. Billy immediately noticed he had a British accent. 'And I don't want any trouble with any of you, or the big guys.' He eyed the dragons suspiciously. 'I'm here because I'm looking for my mum.'

Whatever Billy had been expecting the boy to say, it wasn't that.

'Your mum?' he repeated. 'As in your mom? Your mother?'

'Yeah,' said Jordan. 'My mum.'

'What in the world is your mom doing in the Dragon Realm?' said Charlotte. She leaped off Tank and landed next to Billy and Jordan. 'And how did you even get in here?'

Jordan shrugged. 'I don't know what she's doing here. I just know she's in here somewhere. She researches portals into other worlds – real sci-fi type stuff. I never thought she'd actually make one. But she did. In our kitchen.' He shook his head as if he still couldn't quite believe it. 'She doesn't even like cooking! But one minute, she was leaning over the stove, and that should have been my first clue something was off, and the next, well, she was sucked into this huge, swirling hole. So I followed her. But I clearly didn't move fast enough, or something, because when I got sucked into this place, I couldn't see her. Or anyone. At least not until now.' He glanced at the dragons with a mix of awe and fear. 'Oh, also, my mum does research on you guys. On dragons, I mean.'

'Is that why you're so calm?' said Billy. 'Because your mom researches dragons?'

Jordan let out a nervous laugh. 'Oh, I'm not calm. I feel as if I might wet myself. But I'm glad you think that.'

'Don't worry,' said Ling-Fei. 'You're safer now that you've found us.'

'If you say so,' said Jordan sceptically.

'I'm fascinated that humans do research on us. How delightful!' said Buttons. He landed with an elegant thump on the ground. 'You must think us frightfully rude not to introduce ourselves. I'm Buttons. This is my human, Dylan.'

From his perch on Buttons's back, Dylan groaned. 'That makes me sound like your pet.' Then he slid off and nodded in greeting at Jordan. 'Hello,' he said. 'It's nice to meet someone from this side of the Atlantic! Let me guess, London?'

'How could you tell?'

'I've been to London once or twice,' Dylan said proudly.

'Where are the rest of you from?' Jordan asked, looking around. 'And, um ... why are you all here? And where am I?'

'Slow down, cowboy. We're the ones doing the questioning,' said Charlotte, hands on her hips. 'But I suppose we can tell you our names. It's the polite thing to do, as Buttons pointed out. I'm Charlotte Bell. This is my dragon, Tank.'

Tank snorted in greeting, a wisp of smoke coming out from one of his huge nostrils.

Ling-Fei waved from her perch on Xing's back. 'I'm Ling-Fei. The dragon who picked you up is Xing. She's not as mean as she seems, I promise.'

'Are we sure the human boy is trustworthy?' said Xing, eyeing Jordan suspiciously. 'Two new human children in one day! We are not babysitters.'

'Well, lucky for you, we aren't babies,' said Billy. 'And he seems trustworthy to me.' Billy couldn't help but imagine what it would be like if he was on his own, trying to find his mom. It made him want to help Jordan.

'No offence, Billy, but your sense of who's trustworthy isn't always totally on point,' said Charlotte. 'I mean, I know we trust Spark *now* . . .'

Billy bristled. 'That was different!' His dragon, Spark, had tricked them all into believing she wasn't descending into a dark magic addiction. But Billy had felt the most betrayed, the most tricked, because he was the closest to her. It had felt as if his very soul had been ripped in two when he had realized the depth of her betrayal. But she'd come back, stronger and better and more true than before. He still didn't like thinking about that time though. He had forgiven Spark completely, but it still hurt to remember.

'That *was* different,' said Spark. 'And I agree with Billy. This boy, Jordan, has a good heart. You cannot all sense it?'

'Children usually do have good hearts,' Xing said begrudgingly.

'What about my heart?' piped up Lola. 'Do I have a good heart?'

Spark smiled at Lola. 'Your heart practically glows with goodness. Whatever dragon you bond with will have a very good heart indeed.'

Jordan perked up. 'Do I get to bond with a dragon too?'

'I thought you wanted to find your mom?' said Billy.

'I mean, can't I do that *and* bond with a dragon?' Jordan grinned for the first time since they'd found him and his silver braces flashed. 'I'd have a better chance of finding my mum if I had a dragon to help me.'

'What happened to you being scared of us?' said Xing with a *harrumph*.

'Oh, don't worry, I'm still mad scared of you,' Jordan said, and Billy found himself grinning at the new boy.

When Billy had first come into the Dragon Realm, he'd had his friends by his side. This boy had arrived on his own, and Billy was impressed by the bravery that took. But he also knew how dangerous it was here. And more than that, they didn't have time to go searching for a rogue human in the Dragon Realm. Even one who apparently had the skill and power to open a portal.

'This is a huge realm,' Billy said to Jordan. 'It could take you days, weeks, maybe even months to find your mom. You should go home.' Even as he said the words, he knew Jordan was determined to stay, with or without their help.

Jordan gave an exaggerated look over both his shoulders. 'And tell me exactly how I'm supposed to do that? That swirling thing in my kitchen sucked me up and spat me out, and I don't know how to get back, even if I wanted to go home without my mum. Which I don't want to do. I'm not leaving here without her.'

Billy sighed. He'd do the same if it were his mom, dad or brother. Or anyone he cared about.

'We can't just let him roam the Dragon Realm on his own,' said Ling-Fei, her forehead creasing with worry. 'He'll never survive.'

'Hey! I'm not that useless,' Jordan said.

'It is more dangerous here than you know,' Tank said in a low rumble.

'That's why I have to find my mum,' Jordan said firmly. 'She's here alone.' He paused. 'Although she does have a sword.'

'A sword?' said Charlotte. 'Now I'm intrigued.'

'Your mum doesn't sound anything like my mum,' said Dylan. 'She opened a portal in your kitchen and she has a sword. Are you sure she isn't a super villain?'

'Trust me, my mum is one of the good guys,' said Jordan. 'And the sword is from her work or something.' He scrunched his face up. 'It has a funny name.'

The four dragons stilled.

'The sword has a name?' said Spark. Her voice was calm, but Billy heard the unease in it.

'Do you know what it's called?' said Buttons.

'San ... san something,' said Jordan. 'San glad? San dio?' He shook his head. 'No, that isn't it.'

'*Sanguinem gladio.*' Tank's voice echoed all around them. 'The sword is called *sanguinem gladio.*'

'Yes! That's it!' said Jordan.

The dragons all exchanged a look.

'What?' said Billy, trying to push back the rising anxiety inside him. He could tell the dragons were alarmed, and *that* alarmed him.

Buttons sighed deeply. 'If his mother does indeed have the *sanguinem gladio*, well, that changes everything.'

No Ordinary Sword

'It is no ordinary sword,' said Spark, her voice solemn.

'Of course it isn't,' muttered Dylan. 'Why would it be an ordinary sword?' Then his eyes lit up. 'Wait! I know what it means! It's Latin, isn't it?'

Billy remembered that Dylan loved languages – it was part of the reason he'd wanted to go to Camp Dragon in the first place, so he could study Mandarin.

'It is indeed,' said Buttons proudly. 'Well done.'

'Yes, yes, gold star for Dylan. Are you going to tell the rest of us what it means?' said Charlotte. Billy could tell she wished she were the one who knew what it meant – she prided herself on being the one who knew all the answers.

Dylan scrunched his face up. 'Well, it isn't an exact translation, but I'll do my best ...'

Billy grinned at his friend. 'Dylan, just tell us what it means.'

'The Blood Sword,' he said slowly. The words sent a shiver down Billy's spine, and he looked up at Spark. 'Is that really the name of the sword?'

Spark nodded. 'It is as close to a translation as the human tongue can come. It is a very old and ancient sword. I thought it had disappeared thousands of years ago.'

'And, er ...' Billy cleared his throat. 'Why is it called the Blood Sword?'

'As Spark said, it is no ordinary sword,' said Tank. 'The *sanguinem gladio* is the sword that slayed the first dragon.'

'The first *ever* dragon?' repeated Ling-Fei.

'Yes. An incredibly old and powerful dragon. Portals between the realms have always existed, and humans and dragons have always found each other. For a long time, they existed in peace. It was only after this dragon, the Glorious Old, was slayed that humans realized it was possible to kill a dragon, and the dragons wanted revenge. It changed everything.'

'But why would someone want to kill a dragon?' said Lola, shaking her head. 'I've only just seen dragons for the first time, but you're all magnificent!'

'Thank you,' said Xing primly. 'The Glorious Old was killed for the same reason humans, or dragons for that matter, ever want to do anything. For power. The man who slayed this dragon did so because he thought he would inherit the dragon's power.'

'And did he?' said Jordan, his voice a high squeak.

'No,' said Billy slowly, even though he didn't know the story. 'It doesn't work like that. The best way for a dragon, and a human, to gain power is for them to share a heart bond. Killing a dragon just gives you a dead dragon.' He shuddered. He couldn't imagine how awful it would feel to kill a dragon.

'Billy is right,' said Buttons. 'Dragons have the ability to use dark magic to take power from one another, and from humans and all living things, by draining life force. But it's not something humans can do.'

'Of course they still try,' said Xing dismissively. 'But no human-made sword could ever slay a dragon.'

'However *sanguinem gladio* is not human-made,' said Tank. 'It was forged and found. Much like the eight pearls, nobody knows for sure where the sword comes from, but we believe they share the same power source. Legend tells of a hidden fountain known as the Forbidden Fountain. From the Forbidden Fountain supposedly pours the golden elixir, a substance so powerful that it can create and imbue objects with their own immense power. The *sanguinem gladio* is one such item.'

'It is said the *sanguinem gladio* can cut anything,' said Buttons. 'It was so powerful that after it was used to slay the Glorious Old, another group of dragons hid the sword where it could not be found.'

'But obviously someone did find it,' said Billy. He swivelled his gaze to Jordan. 'You've seen this thing?'

Jordan shrugged. 'I've seen a super old sword that my mum calls the *sanguinem gladio*. It might not actually be the same sword. Lots of swords could have that name, right?'

'It is highly unlikely,' said Xing. She flew closer to Jordan, putting her face right next to his. Jordan stiffened, but held his ground. 'Tell me, boy from England, what is it your mother does?'

'I told you,' said Jordan. 'She does research on

portals and dragons. But she also studies really old artefacts.'

'Whom does she work for?' said Buttons. 'That may give us more insight into how she found herself in possession of such an extraordinary item.'

'She started a new job last year. She was a university researcher for a long time, but they closed her department. It was awful. She was out of work for months and we ended up having to move. But then she got a call from this big international company called TURBO, and they were looking for someone who was an expert in her exact field. They offered to pay Mum double what she was making before. It felt too good to be true.' Jordan sighed glumly. 'And now it looks as if it was. A few days ago I overheard a call she had with her boss, this rich guy named Frank Albert who runs TURBO. The first time I met him, he was all smiles, but I could tell they were fake. I've never liked him. And then on the call I heard him shouting at my mum. Now I really don't like him.'

'What was the fight about?' said Ling-Fei gently.

'My mum kept saying that things had gone too far

and they had to put "it" back.' Jordan scratched his head. 'Maybe she meant the sword?'

'I think I've heard of TURBO,' said Dylan. 'I've seen their adverts. They always use words like "innovate" and "discover" and "science" in bold letters, but they never tell you what they actually do.' He looked at Jordan. 'Do you know?'

Jordan shrugged. 'I'm not sure. Some kind of tech company, or maybe medicine? Or both? I didn't really care what they did – I was just happy because my mum was happy.' Then he sighed and shook his head. 'Or at least she was until she got into that fight with her boss. For the past few days she's been super tense and jumpy. Then she disappeared into the portal, and now I don't know what to do.'

'You are a good son,' said Tank unexpectedly. 'You care for your mother's well-being, and you have followed her in here, into the dangerous unknown, to help her.'

Jordan glanced at his feet, obviously embarrassed by the praise. 'This is a weird day,' he said. 'I'm still not sure if I'm awake or dreaming.'

'Welcome to the club!' said Lola.

Dylan laughed. 'I *still* feel like that.'

'If your mother does indeed have the *sanguinem gladio*, we must find her. If the sword falls into the wrong hands, the results could be catastrophic,' said Xing.

'Hey! My mum is trustworthy,' said Jordan defensively.

'Of course,' said Buttons. 'But someone else, someone untrustworthy, could take the sword from her.'

Something occurred to Billy. 'Did you say that your mom and her boss were arguing just a few days ago?'

Jordan nodded.

Billy turned to Spark. 'And things started disappearing here a few days ago too, right?'

'Yes,' said Spark, tilting her head quizzically.

'Well,' said Billy, his words tumbling out all in a rush, 'maybe it's all connected. The sword, the disappearing mountains, the sea dragon. Someone in the Human Realm has a sword that has been hidden for thousands of years in the Dragon Realm. That would definitely have some sort of impact, wouldn't it?'

'And didn't you say that the sword could cut through anything, Buttons?' added Ling-Fei. 'What if the sword is cutting holes between the realms? And that's how the sea dragon Billy saw came through into the Human Realm?'

'Could it be?' said Buttons, eyes widening. 'The *sanguinem gladio* is indeed immensely powerful, but a power of that magnitude ...' His voice trailed off as the dragons all pondered what Ling-Fei was suggesting.

'It is possible,' said Spark. 'All the more reason for us to find Jordan's mother.'

'So you'll help me?' said Jordan, his voice brightening.

'I suppose now we have no choice,' said Xing, flicking her tail in annoyance.

'But what about everything happening in the Human Realm?' said Charlotte. She glanced uneasily at the others. 'I'm worried about my family. If things in this realm are impacting our world, well, we need to stop it.'

'And finding the sword is the first step,' said Billy. He looked at Charlotte sympathetically. 'I get it. I'm worried about my family too. Especially since I saw that sea dragon so close to where we live.'

'How do you think I feel?' chimed in Lola. 'I didn't even leave my mom a note! She's going to be so worried.'

'Spark can take you home,' Billy offered, but Lola shook her head.

'No. I want to help. This is worth getting into trouble for. I didn't come all this way just to turn around and go home.'

Part of Billy wanted to say that he wasn't sure how much Lola actually could help when she didn't have any powers or even a dragon she was bonded with, but he also knew they needed all the help they could get.

'It was one thing when we were battling evil dragons in this realm,' said Dylan, 'but knowing that dangerous things are happening back home is even scarier.'

They were all quiet for a moment.

'We always stick together, right?' said Billy. The others nodded. Billy looked at Jordan and Lola. 'If you two are doing this with us, you're part of our team now. Are you in?'

'I've been in since the moment I saw that sea dragon,' said Lola.

'And I've been in since I followed my mum through the portal in our kitchen,' added Jordan.

'Great,' said Billy. 'Now the only thing left to do is figure out which dragon you two should ride on.'

'I can most certainly carry three humans, but I do not think it will be necessary,' said Spark. 'It appears we have company.' She lifted her head to the sky, where three magnificent dragons were flying towards them.

'Is it good company or bad company?' said Jordan.

'Oh, it's very good company,' said Charlotte.

Despite all of his anxiety, Billy's face split into a wide grin. 'It's the Thunder Clan.'

A Hard Choice

The three Thunder Clan dragons landed gracefully next to Billy and the others. The smallest dragon, a young, dark blue dragon with giant horns on her head, squealed in delight.

'Billy! Charlotte! Dylan! Ling-Fei! And other humans! This is such a happy surprise!' The tiny gold flying pig hovering next to her oinked in agreement.

'Midnight! And Goldie!' Billy couldn't stop beaming. He hadn't expected to see Midnight, and his spirits had instantly lifted at the arrival of the young dragon. He threw his arms around her, careful of her horns. 'I'm so glad to see you both!' He looked up at the other two dragons and bowed his head respectfully. 'You too, Thunder and Lightning.'

The largest of the dragons, Thunder, a huge, black dragon with a long, flowing, white moustache, let out a low rumbling laugh. 'Well, this is an unexpected reunion. We did not think you would be back in our realm so soon.'

Next to him, Lightning, a sparkling dragon covered in scales made up of hundreds of shifting colours, nodded hello. 'While I am also glad to see all of you, I am worried the reason for your return is not a good one. We saw the mountains disappear on our flight here. We've been exploring the realm to try to see how far the disappearances stretch, and we can now say with certainty that it is happening more and more across the entire realm. I live in fear that we will be in the wrong place at the wrong time and be pulled into a soft spot.'

'It is an understandable fear,' said Spark. 'Keep Midnight close. We do not know what is causing the soft spots, and until we do, it is wise to be wary.'

'And it is not just our realm that has been affected,' added Tank. 'There are reports of strange occurrences in the Human Realm.'

'Is that why the children have returned?' said Thunder.

'Yes,' said Billy. 'We think everything is connected.' He quickly told the Thunder Clan about the sea dragon, and the weird things that had been happening all over the Human Realm. When he got to the part about the sword, Thunder and Lightning both gasped.

'Your mother carries the *sanguinem gladio*?' said Thunder, his giant, furry eyebrows knitting together in worry as he looked at Jordan.

'Er, I think so?' said Jordan, shifting his weight from foot to foot. 'I didn't realize what a big deal it was.'

'Are there many magical swords hanging around your house?' said Dylan.

Jordan laughed. 'No, but my mum is always bringing home weird stuff for her research.'

'It is imperative that we find the sword,' said Lightning, 'And as soon as possible.'

'We need a plan,' said Billy.

'Your favourite four words,' said Dylan with a grin.

Billy elbowed his friend. 'It's true! We *do* need a plan.' Then he swallowed. 'Does anyone have any ideas?'

'Well,' said Ling-Fei softly, 'Xing and I can help to find the sword. We can sense magic, remember?'

'You can do *what*?' said Jordan.

'Seriously, you're standing next to seven dragons, and that's the thing you find unbelievable?' said Charlotte.

'Dragons are meant to be magical. But you ... you're just a kid,' said Jordan, still staring at Ling-Fei.

'When we bonded with our dragons, we also gained powers,' said Billy, as casually as he could. 'There were some magic pearls involved ...'

'Those pearls are the ones we suspect came from the same place as the *sanguinem gladio*,' said Tank.

'Anyway, the point is, now we have some lingering ... superpowers,' Billy finished.

Lola gaped at him. 'Is that why you're such a good surfer?'

'I was a good surfer before this,' said Billy with a grin. 'But having super-enhanced speed and agility helps a little bit.' It was true. When Billy had found the Lightning Pearl, he'd been gifted with the ability to move at super speeds, and he'd become much more aware of his surroundings. Without the pearl itself, his power had weakened, but it wasn't gone entirely.

'Just a bit,' said Charlotte with a snort. 'And if you're impressed with that, well, wait until you hear what I can do. I've got super strength.' The pearls had unlocked and enhanced innate skills that they already had, and strength had come naturally to Charlotte. At one point after she'd got her power from the Gold Pearl, she had been strong enough to hold open the Earth itself. Without her pearl, her strength had diminished significantly, but she was still able to lift a car in the air.

'Oi! Hold on. Mine is pretty good. Charm is its own kind of strength,' said Dylan. His ability to charm people, and dragons, had become so powerful at one point that he'd been able to make his friends seem invisible, all by the power of suggestion. Then he frowned. 'Although mine seems to come and go more than the others.'

'They've all been a bit unpredictable recently,' said Ling-Fei. 'Although, I feel like my power is coming back, even without my Jade Pearl. Isn't that strange?'

'Me too,' said Charlotte.

Billy frowned and looked at Spark. 'Could that be connected with . . . everything else?'

'It is entirely possible,' said Spark.

'The longer that the *sanguinem gladio* is unaccounted for, the more unstable things will become,' said Xing. 'Which reminds me. We are wasting time talking about the sword when we should be looking for it.'

'Then we are decided,' said Tank.

Billy took a deep breath and grinned at the group. 'Time to find that sword.'

Diamond Formation

'We have no time to waste.'

Xing's words echoed in the early morning air. In the distance, behind the soft spot where the mountain range had disappeared, the orange, oval-shaped sun of the Dragon Realm was beginning to rise. The three moons stayed fixed, as always.

Billy wondered if the sun and the moons could fall into a soft spot and be pulled into the Human Realm. What would happen if there were suddenly multiple suns in the sky?

Xing was right – they had to hurry.

He looked over at Thunder, Lightning and Midnight. 'Will you help us?'

'Of course,' said Midnight, who was so excited she started flying figures of eight in the air right above them.

'You are part of our clan now. For ever,' added Thunder.

Billy felt his cheeks flush at the praise. He felt lucky. He had his human family, and now he had his dragon family too.

'While I certainly can carry all of you,' said Spark, 'it might be wiser to have everyone on their own dragon.'

Midnight paused in between loops. 'Oh, let me carry a human! Please, please, please!'

'Midnight, if you carry one of the human children, you will have to fly very carefully,' said Lightning.

'I can do it,' said Midnight. She landed next to Jordan and pointed a wing at him. 'You. I have a good feeling about you. Come with me!'

Jordan gave her a small smile, his braces glinting. 'All right,' he said shyly. He slowly reached out and stroked Midnight behind her horns, and she tossed her head back and forth in pleasure.

Billy watched with amazement as a small, gold

spark lit up in Midnight's chest. Was it possible that Jordan was Midnight's heart bond dragon? How could that be? But then the gold spark faded, and Billy thought that perhaps he had imagined it.

'What about me?' said Lola. 'Who do I get to fly on?'

'I'll carry you,' said Lightning, lowering herself to the ground so Lola could climb on. 'You'll have to hold tight. Without the heart bond, you'll slip off more easily.'

'And I will fly behind, keeping an eye out for danger,' said Thunder. 'Midnight, if you tire, let me know, and I will take the boy.'

'I won't get tired,' said Midnight. 'I never get tired!'

'You do seem to have endless energy,' said Spark with a smile at the young dragon. 'You remind me of myself when I was young.'

'I wish I had known you then,' said Billy, imagining a smaller, younger Spark. One who was as carefree as Midnight.

'One day,' said Spark, 'I will tell you all about when I was a hatchling. But today is not that day. Today we must focus on the task ahead of us.' She turned her attention to Jordan.

'Jordan,' she said gently. 'You will have the strongest pull towards your mother. You must focus as hard on her as you can. Think of her face; think of what you love about her. That will guide you.'

'And Ling-Fei and I will focus our attention on the sword itself. As a seeker dragon, I am drawn to powerful things,' said Xing.

'Don't worry,' said Ling-Fei with a smile. 'We'll find your mom.'

'If she truly has the sword, others will be looking for her,' said Spark. 'Anything that powerful will draw dragons and other beings to her like a beacon. But we have you, Jordan. And you will guide us to her.'

Jordan nodded, and Billy didn't miss how his fists clenched at his side in determination.

'Hop on!' said Midnight, and Jordan carefully clambered onto Midnight's back and found his seat.

'Whoa,' he said, eyes widening. 'This is . . .'

'Awesome!' cried Lola from her perch on Lightning's back. 'I don't think I'll ever get used to it!'

'Stay alert; stay focused. We will find Jordan's mother, and we will find the sword,' said Spark.

'Then we'll go home and fix whatever is going on,' said Billy with more confidence than he felt.

'That's the spirit,' said Ling-Fei. Then she looked back at Midnight. 'Midnight, do you think you can keep up with Xing? You should probably fly at the front with us so we can work together.'

'And the rest of us will go in two-eyed diamond formation,' said Spark. 'Billy and I will take the right flank, Lightning the left and Thunder will be the final point. Buttons and Tank will fly out of formation so they can focus on watching for anything strange. If we sense any danger, Midnight will fall back behind Xing so she will be protected in the middle of us all.'

Lightning nodded. 'Thank you,' she said. 'That makes me feel much better.' As Midnight's mother, she was especially protective of the young dragon.

'I can take care of myself!' said Midnight indignantly. 'I don't need to be treated like a hatchling!'

'Midnight,' Thunder said sternly. 'You are the youngest. You are lucky we are allowing you to fly at all. Do not make me change my mind and find a mountain for us all to hide in.'

'I have hidden enough for a lifetime,' said Lightning. Back in Dragon City, Lightning had hidden her immense power from the Dragon of Death by going into a deep slumber, never leaving the marble orb that had been the Thunder Clan's home. 'We stay safe, we stay together, but we stay in the sky.'

'We probably shouldn't stay in any one place for too long,' said Billy, eyeing where the mountain range had been. 'Who knows what else could turn into a soft spot?'

'Seriously,' said Charlotte, 'I have no interest in getting sucked into who knows where.'

'Same here,' said Dylan. 'At least if we're in the air, we're safe, right?'

'We can't know for sure,' admitted Buttons. 'We've never seen anything like this before in all our time in this realm.'

'We must be alert,' thundered Tank. 'Fly close; fly fast.'

And with that, the group of seven dragons, six human children and one tiny gold flying pig took off into the dawn.

*

Billy felt a strange sense of helplessness as they flew.

When Dylan had been taken and they'd had to search for him, they'd felt drawn to him through their friendship, and they'd used that connection to help guide them. And when they'd been separated from their dragons, Billy's bond with Spark had helped lead him to them.

But he felt no connection at all to Jordan's mother, or the sword that the dragons sought.

Billy? Spark's voice echoed in his mind. *I am sensing an anxiousness from you. Is everything all right?* She paused. *I mean with you. I do realize that both of the realms seem to be in great danger.*

Billy couldn't help but smile. *I'm fine*, he thought back. *Just feeling a little useless. I want to help, but I don't know how.*

Speak to the boy, said Spark through their bond. *You know how frightened he must be.*

And before Billy could respond, Spark shifted her course slightly so she was flying closer to Midnight, close enough that Billy could talk to Jordan.

He expected to see Jordan clutching Midnight, sitting stiffly so he wouldn't fall off, but instead Jordan seemed remarkably relaxed, and also very secure in his perch on Midnight's back. In contrast, Lola had both arms wrapped tightly around Lightning's neck, and she hadn't moved position since they took off. Goldie seemed to have taken to Lola and flew next to her, squeaking reassuringly.

Midnight was chattering away, as always. Billy caught the last part of a story she was telling. 'And then I burst into the train and said, "I KNEW IT!"'

Billy couldn't help but smile. She was telling the story of when she had discovered their secret hiding spot in Dragon City. That was when they had decided they could trust her.

'And then what happened?' asked Jordan.

'And then she nearly blew the roof off our train carriage. Watch out for her horns when they get red,' said Billy with a grin.

At the mention of her horns, they did indeed start to change from a glowing gold to a faint ember red.

'Steady on,' said Jordan in a slight panic, and to Billy's amazement, Midnight's horns returned to gold.

'I saved you!' said Midnight. 'Without me, they would have been caught by the Dragon of Death.'

Jordan let out a low whistle. 'You lot have had some mad adventures,' he said. 'It's going to be hard to go back to my real life after I know all this is out here.'

'You can just come and visit us!' said Midnight. 'Like Billy and the others do. Although they haven't been back in *so* long!' She gave Billy a reproachful look.

Billy laughed. 'It's only been a few weeks since we left camp! And it isn't that easy to pop in and out of the Dragon Realm, you know!'

'My mum made it look pretty easy,' said Jordan. 'She just brewed up a portal in our kitchen and then she was gone.' He shook his head in awe.

'Well, it usually isn't easy to get into this realm,' said Billy. And as glad as he was that they had been able to return without any issues, he knew it meant something was off. Spark shouldn't have been able to make portals that quickly or easily. He couldn't shake the feeling that the missing sword had something to do with it.

'My mum isn't going to believe this,' said Jordan. 'Me. Riding a dragon.'

'If your mother truly has the *sanguinem gladio* and created a portal in your kitchen, I suspect she will be used to believing unbelievable things,' said Spark.

'I just hope we find her soon,' Jordan said anxiously.

'We will.' Billy spoke with as much confidence as he could muster. 'How are you feeling? Does it feel as if we're still going in the right direction? As if we're getting closer to her?'

Jordan scrunched his face up in concentration. 'I don't know. I'm trying as best I can, I really am. But it's hard to focus on this *pull* to my mum when I'm riding a dragon. I'm scared about falling off.'

'Oh, don't worry about that!' chirped Midnight. 'I won't let you fall.'

'You do look very comfortable riding Midnight,' said Ling-Fei, glancing over her shoulder from where she rode with Xing. 'Do you horseback ride or something?'

Jordan scoffed. 'Do you think everyone in England rides around on ponies?'

Ling-Fei laughed. 'Fair point.' Then her gaze softened. 'If it helps, both Xing and I are feeling drawn towards a strong magical source in this direction. We don't know for sure if it's the sword, but there's *something* in this area that's sending out a strong magical pulse.'

'I really hope it's the sword and not ... something else,' said Billy. 'I don't really want to come up against a surprise super-powerful, magical creature that we weren't expecting.'

Jordan raised his eyebrows. 'We're flying with seven dragons. I'd bet on us being able to beat anything we run into.'

'While I appreciate your confidence in us, we're in a realm *full* of dragons,' said Billy. 'And all kinds of other creatures we definitely don't want to meet.'

'Like what?' said Jordan.

'Rock trolls, giant crabs, screaming serpents, huge scorpions, fish that can swallow you whole, gigantic worms ...' Ling-Fei's voice trailed off. 'What am I missing?'

'Whatever that thing is up there,' said Billy with a gulp, pointing ahead where a buzzing swarm of hundreds of small, winged creatures was flying straight towards them.

Dragobees

The buzzing swarm hurtled towards the diamond dragon formation.

'Get back!' roared Tank.

'And stay together!' cried Buttons.

'What are those things?' Billy shouted as the Thunder Clan, Spark, Xing, Buttons and Tank drew closer together, making sure Midnight was in the centre and well protected. Billy sensed Spark preparing for an attack.

'Dragobees,' said Spark grimly. 'A type of very small, but very aggressive dragon that is always found in large numbers. On their own, they are easy to defeat, but as a swarm, they can be deadly.'

'So, like . . . killer dragonflies?' said Billy, straining his eyes to try to make out the individual dragons in the swarm. At this distance, they still looked like a massive shifting cloud of shining scales and wings. But as they grew closer, he noticed individual creatures in the mass. They were about fifteen centimetres long, with long snouts and thrashing spiked tails.

'Dragonflies are insects. A dragobee is a deadly type of dragon,' said Xing. 'Do not underestimate them, and whatever you do, do not let them sting or bite you. Once one does, it will send a paralysing venom through you, and you will be unable to fight back. The rest of the swarm will smell the venom and descend on you so they can devour you alive.'

Billy shuddered as the swarm moved as one, forming different shapes as they drew nearer.

'Are those small dragons trying to make themselves look like one big dragon?' said Lola. Billy realized she was right – they had formed the shape of a much larger dragon, one that roughly resembled the shape and size of Lightning.

'Yes,' said Lightning. 'And it appears they will be coming for me first.'

'Not if I have anything to do about it,' roared Thunder. Before Billy realized what he was doing, Thunder flew above the diamond formation and shot a huge stream of fire directly at the dragobee swarm. Tank followed, blowing a huge fireball towards them.

But the dragobees were fast. They split into two new dragon shapes, and Thunder's and Tank's fire only caught a few on the edge of the swarm. The dragobees' buzzing grew louder, and more incessant.

'Well, now you have made them angry,' said Xing. 'Brute strength will not win in a battle against dragobees. You should know that.'

'We did not have such creatures back in Dragon City,' said Thunder as he returned to his place in the formation.

'Tank really should know better though,' said Buttons.

'It was worth a try,' huffed Tank.

'These things are gross!' cried Charlotte. 'I don't want to get anywhere near them.'

Then the dragobees changed shape again, this time long and slender, like Xing.

'Oh, the silly little things think they can get me,' said Xing. Her teeth flashed as she bared them in warning. 'Spark, watch my back!'

Xing flew so fast that she became barely more than a silver blur streaking through the sky. Billy held his breath as he watched, terrified that even with the heart bond, Ling-Fei would fall off.

But she didn't, even as Xing flew round and round the dragobees so quickly she created a vortex of wind and they began to separate, turning from one large shape into individual small dragons. Dragons so small that Xing could easily knock them out of the sky with a swift hit of her tail.

Suddenly, Billy saw a group of dragobees at the back break off and form a new swarm, one shaped like a giant stinger.

'Spark!' he cried. 'Get that swarm!'

Spark was already racing through the air, her horns crackling with electricity as she shot out a stream of lightning towards the new swarm. It struck true and the swarm dissolved.

The dragobees roared their frustration and began to regroup.

'It's as if they're multiplying!' said Billy. He couldn't understand how they were still battling them.

'They very well may be,' said Spark. It was true – more and more swarms seemed to be coming out of the air, each new swarm targeting one of the larger dragons until Midnight was the only one not fighting a swarm. But with all the other dragons battling, she was exposed in the centre of the diamond formation.

Billy realized this at the same moment two of the larger swarms did. They turned in sync, changed shape to form one giant mouth, jaw gaping, and came chomping towards Midnight.

'Midnight! Move!' screamed Lightning, turning to get to her, but the swarm surrounding Lightning turned into a net, making it impossible for her to break through.

Thunder roared and flew towards Midnight, but he was too far away. The dragobee swarm was already there, and Midnight seemed petrified. Her wings were flapping to keep her in the air, but she wasn't attempting to dodge the attack. Her eyes were huge as she stared at the mouth coming to devour her.

'No!' yelled Billy, urging Spark towards Midnight. 'Do something, Spark! Shoot electricity!'

'We have to be careful,' said Spark as she flew closer. 'I do not want to accidentally hit Midnight.'

Midnight was fully surrounded now, so much so that Billy could barely see her and Jordan. Then, to Billy's astonishment, through the dragobees' rapidly fluttering wings, he saw Jordan stand up on Midnight's back and wave his arms at the swarm.

They paused, seemingly confused, but within seconds the dragobees descended on Jordan, covering his arms and legs. Billy watched on in horror as Jordan screamed and then went completely stiff.

'Jordan!' Billy shouted. He urged Spark forward, but the swarms were blocking them and there was no way of breaking through.

Then, as if in slow motion, Jordan slid off Midnight and plummeted to the ground below.

Midnight Fights Back

The swarms of dragobees all moved as one, pulling back from the dragons they were battling and focusing all of their attention on Jordan. Billy knew that they smelled the paralysing venom in his blood and that it would send an irresistible signal to them. They would want to reach him before he hit the ground so they could devour him while he still lived. The dragobees regrouped, forming one giant dragon, almost as large as Tank, and dived after Jordan's falling body.

But Billy and Spark were faster. Billy used all of his energy to focus on his bond with Spark, urging her faster, channelling his own power of speed into her. Her wings were flush against her body and she was entirely vertical, her snout pointed directly at the ground, with Billy pressed flat against her back. They went so fast that tears streamed from his eyes, but still they dived.

Right before Jordan hit the ground, Spark swooped over him and caught him with her claws, like an eagle catching prey.

'Billy! Grab him!' she shouted as she flung Jordan up towards where Billy was sitting. With his reawakened agility power and heightened sense of movement around him, Billy knew where Jordan was going to be and reached out to grab his wrists, pulling him up onto Spark's back.

Jordan still couldn't move, but his eyes were wide and terrified.

The dragobees roared in unison and descended on them. There were thousands of them, and they were so close that Billy could see their sharp teeth and long tongues.

A clear, high-pitched voice broke through the buzzing of the dragobees. 'GET AWAY FROM MY HUMAN!'

Midnight barrelled towards the swarm, vibrating

with anger, horns glowing molten red. A huge blast of energy exploded out of her horns, so strong that for a moment the entire world went still, as if time itself had stopped, and then the blast hit the dragobee swarm. The swarm exploded and dragobees were sent flying through the air until only a few dazed ones remained, who quickly flew off to find the others. Billy felt his jaw drop. He had no idea that Midnight was so powerful.

'I'll get the stragglers!' roared Tank, and he and Charlotte took off after the remaining dragobees.

Spark landed as gently as she could on the ground, and the other dragons followed. Billy still held the wrists of a not-moving Jordan, but he was awake and breathing, which was a good sign.

Midnight landed with a thump next to Spark. 'Is he alive?'

Billy nodded. He looked up at Buttons. 'But he could use your help.' Buttons was a healer dragon, with the ability to recharge and heal humans and dragons alike.

Buttons waddled over and took a look at Jordan. 'I'll do my best, but the stings look serious. They might possibly even be beyond my powers.'

'That doesn't sound good,' Dylan whispered as Buttons began to hum and drum on his stomach. As he did, Billy saw the healing energy flow from Buttons and envelop Jordan.

Midnight hopped around in distress. 'It's my fault! He swatted those dragobees to save me! Did you see? Did you see how he saved me?'

'I did,' said Billy. 'And I saw you save us too. By doing ... whatever it is you just did. I didn't know you *could* do something like that.'

Midnight shrugged. 'I didn't know I could do something like that either!' Her horns were still smoking.

'It was like what you did in the train when we lied to you, but times a million!' said Ling-Fei.

'I think sometimes my emotions explode out of my horns,' said Midnight.

'Well, I know I just met you, but that seems like a good thing! You were the one who got rid of the dragobees!' said Lola, sliding down off Lightning's back.

Lightning hurried to Midnight and nuzzled her. 'What you did was incredibly reckless, but incredibly brave.'

'I wasn't really thinking,' admitted Midnight. 'But I had to do *something*! I felt this pull towards Jordan – to protect him!'

'Interesting,' said Spark, her gaze flicking between Midnight and Jordan. Billy sent her a silent question. *Do you think Midnight could be Jordan's heart bond dragon?*

It is possible. Something like what they did for each other, each protecting the other one, could result in a heart bond. Especially if they have hearts that match.

Thunder lumbered over to Midnight and Lightning. 'Midnight, it is I who should have protected you. I failed to do that. If this human boy had not been so fearless and so brave, I shudder to think about what would have happened. I fear this mission is too dangerous for you.'

'All dragons must learn to fly, and to fight,' said Lightning softly. 'We should be proud of our Midnight.'

'And it is interesting, seeing that the human boy risked his own safety for her,' said Xing.

They all looked at Jordan, but he lay as stiff and silent as a statue. All he did was blink at them.

Buttons exhaled. 'I've done all I can. The boy will live, but to be able to move again, we must seek other ways to heal him.'

Spark stretched her neck out, looking at the land around them. 'Not far from here is a field of flowers and plants known for their healing properties. We can take him there.'

'That will slow us down,' said Xing. 'And we are running out of time. Look there.' She flicked her tail behind her, towards a distant grove of trees. A grove of trees that was shimmering in a way that made Billy feel dizzy. He heard a distant *whoosh*, and then all the trees but one were gone.

Ling-Fei shivered. 'That is unnatural,' she said softly. The rest of the group murmured their agreement.

'Exactly,' said Xing. 'Something is causing those soft spots. And the more I think about it, the more I believe Billy's theory is correct and that it has something to do with the *sanguinem gladio*. We must find the sword, and fast.'

'Without the boy, our chance of finding his mother, and the sword, are slim,' argued Spark.

'I agree with Spark,' said Lightning. 'The boy

should be healed. Not only is it the right thing to do, but he has earned it. His injury is no fault of his own.'

'Of course we have to heal him!' squeaked Midnight. 'I'll fly him there myself!' She paused and looked up at Spark. 'Where exactly are these Healing Fields?'

'We will all go,' said Billy. 'We stay together.' There was a loud oink of agreement next to his ear. Billy turned and smiled at the sight of the tiny gold flying pig hovering over his shoulder. 'There you are, Goldie! I'm glad you're all right.' He held out his hand for the pig, who curled up in his palm and started snoring.

'Of course the pig is all right – it is immortal,' said Xing. 'And it could certainly help a bit more in our battles.' She glared at the pig, who continued to snore in blissful ignorance. Billy slipped Goldie into a pocket on the chest of his super-suit. He would never admit it to Xing, but he felt as if the tiny gold flying pig was a good luck charm. 'If we are going to stay together and head to the Healing Fields,' Xing continued, 'we should go quickly. I will lead the way.'

Lola raised her hand as if she were in school. 'Can I ask a question?'

Xing let out an exasperated sigh. 'That *is* a question. What is it?'

'I realize that we're in a very big hurry, and also that we need to get Jordan to the Healing Fields as soon as possible, but what are the chances of us finding something to eat?' She shrugged apologetically as she looked over at Billy. 'Dinner at your house seems like a very long time ago.'

Billy's stomach growled at the thought of the meal. Lola was right – it had been hours and hours since they'd eaten. Or slept. A wave of fatigue washed over him.

'The girl is right,' said Spark. 'We cannot force the children to keep going without food or rest.'

'We can all rest at the Healing Fields,' said Lightning.

'And I will find food,' added Thunder.

'Humans and their never-ending need for food,' said Xing dismissively. 'Fine. We will rest. But as soon as the boy is healed and can help lead us towards his mother, we will not stop until we have found the *sanguinem gladio*.'

'Find the sword, save both realms, go home,' said Billy. 'Sounds like my kind of plan.'

'I just hope everything is okay at home,' said Ling-Fei uneasily, glancing at the still-shimmering spot where the trees once stood.

'Me too,' said Billy. The drama of the dragobees had pushed thoughts of home and his family out of his mind, but now his worries came rushing back. What if more dragons somehow ended up in the Human Realm? Or other creatures like the dragobees? They had to get to the bottom of what was happening, and fast.

The Great Four

The dragons returned to diamond formation, but this time Jordan flew on Thunder's back. Midnight had tried to argue that she could carry Jordan on her own, but while the paralysing venom was still in his blood, he couldn't even sit up. Thunder's moustache was so long, he was able to loop it behind his head, like reins, and secure it around Jordan's waist, so he couldn't fall off the huge dragon.

Billy silently wondered if the suspected bond between Midnight and Jordan meant that Jordan might have been safer riding Midnight, because the bond would keep him secure. But without confirmation of the heart bond, it was better to be safe, and that meant him flying on Thunder.

Midnight flew right next to her father, keeping an anxious eye on a prone Jordan while chattering away, clearly trying to reassure him that he would be okay. Billy hoped he would be. The distant field of plants and flowers was their last hope of healing him.

They flew on through the late afternoon, Billy growing increasingly aware of how hungry and tired he was. He glanced over at Lola, who was back to holding onto Lightning as if her life depended on it, which Billy figured it actually did.

'Are you okay?' he called out.

'I'm hungry, far from home and I ache all over, but other than that I'm doing good!' she said, flashing him a grin.

'You do not have to hold on quite so tight, you know,' said Lightning gently. 'I can feel how tense you are.'

'I'm not taking any chances,' said Lola. 'What if some other mythical creature appears out of the sky and knocks you off course?'

'I am a very steady flyer,' said Lightning, with a hint of wounded pride.

'It isn't you I'm worried about. It's everything else in this realm.'

'Bet you wish you hadn't come,' Billy said with a laugh.

Lola shook her head, dark hair flying in all directions. 'Are you kidding? I wouldn't miss this for anything! I'm riding a *dragon*!' She beamed. 'You know how, at the start, surfing is super hard? You stand up and fall off the board a million times and you spend most of your time paddling, waiting for a wave? But when it works, it's the best thing ever?'

Billy nodded.

'I figure this is my falling-off-the-board stage. Without actually falling off, of course. Eventually I'll feel more comfortable, right? I mean, look at you! You barely have to hold on!'

Billy didn't want to tell Lola the reason he was able to fly on Spark so easily was because of their heart bond. She was so excited and so hopeful that soon she too would be able to effortlessly fly on the back of a dragon.

'This took some time,' was all he said, but then he grinned. 'It's even better than catching the perfect wave, isn't it?'

'Oh, totally!' Lola gazed down at the ground far beneath them. 'It's the same rush, but better. I'll never, ever forget this.' She looked up at Billy again. 'Thanks for letting me tag along.'

'You didn't give me much of a choice,' said Billy, but he was smiling. If they all survived this, it would be nice to have a friend in his neighbourhood to whom he could talk about everything. Someone who knew what it was like to fly on a dragon.

They flew on, dodging the low floating islands and keeping an eye on the ground below for any unexpected soft spots. Occasionally, they passed other dragons – sometimes they were in small groups, sometimes they were flying alone. Any dragons they saw seemed on edge and alert, but not aggressive. They kept their distance and carried on wherever they were going.

At one point, a dragon with bright, lime green scales and a darker green mane and spikes flew close enough to speak. 'Good day, Spark of Ash.'

Billy felt a thrum go through Spark at hearing the dragon speak that name.

'Good day,' said Spark politely. 'Where do the winds take you?'

'I am flying east. I heard the human children were back. The ones who first came through the mountain.'

'As you can see, that is the case,' said Spark carefully.

'There are whispers of other humans too, grown ones, where humans should not be. And with no dragon guide or guardian.'

Billy sat up with interest. Could that be Jordan's mom? Or someone else? Who else was in the Dragon Realm?

'We seek a grown human who has come to our realm. One who we think may be able to help us fix the soft spots,' Spark spoke politely, but Billy sensed she was wary of this new dragon.

'I wonder if it is humans causing the soft spots,' said the lime green dragon with a sneer.

Xing, who had been flying at the front of the diamond formation but was clearly listening, let out a sharp laugh. 'Humans do not have that kind of power.'

'Good day, Xing who Shines,' said the lime green dragon.

Xing tossed her head at the name. 'You have made it clear you know us . . .'

'All in the realm know you. Both of you, along with Buttons who Heals and Tank who Broke the Tower.' The lime green dragon nodded towards Buttons and Tank. 'Not only for what you did in the time before and the time ahead, but because you have set the new rules. It is because of you that no dragon will swallow a star, or take power where they should not. And for that I thank you.' The lime green dragon dipped its head respectfully, but then glanced back up. 'You have brought peace to our realm, and for that I trust you, but I do not trust humans. Even if they are only children.' Its sharp eyes focused in on Billy and he tensed, suddenly on high alert. He knew from experience that not all dragons were to be trusted either. A rush of protectiveness flowed from Spark through their heart bond, and Billy knew she was thinking the same thing. 'You scoff when I say humans could be the cause of the soft spots, but even if humans do not have that power now, they always covet it. This is how humans are – grasping for power that they do not know what to do with. Power that turns to destruction. It's how they always have been and always will be. It was better when they stayed on their side, and we on ours.'

'Have you flown all this way to lecture us?' said Xing dryly. 'How very boring.'

'I have flown to see if the rumours were true – that the Great Four were on the move, with the Four Children of the Mountain. And I see, like any rumour, it is true, but not true. There are new human children.' The lime green dragon eyed Lola and Jordan curiously. 'And then there are other dragons who fly with you. Ones who also defeated the old Dragon of Death.'

Billy was fascinated that this dragon knew so much. Did all dragons know what had happened back in Dragon City? About him and his friends?

'Yes, curious things are afoot. Or should I say, a-wing?' the dragon continued. 'I wish you well on your quest for the other human you seek, but then I hope to see no more humans here. Humans and dragons are not meant to mix.'

'But the heart bond!' Billy burst out.

'Ah, yes, the heart bond. The thing that connects dragons and humans. The heart bond grants power – dragons have no need of more power, and humans should not have any power at all.'

'You would not speak like that if you had found your heart bond human,' said Spark.

'I have no interest in that. No need for a human. Not now, or ever. Do not worry, I have no nefarious plans for your humans, or any other ones. If they do not bother me, I will not bother them.'

'You are bothering *us* now,' said Tank. 'If you are done, we have wasted enough time listening to your ramblings.'

'Quite right,' said Buttons.

'I have flown alongside you, not slowed you down at all. And look ahead.' The lime green dragon gestured with its round head. 'The Healing Fields are close.' Then it laughed at Billy's expression. 'Do not be so surprised, small human. Your friend, the one who is new, is clearly injured. There is only one place to take him. And to show you how true it is that I mean you no harm, I will also tell you this. Two sunrises ago, two soft spots appeared in the Healing Fields. Be careful where you go.'

And with that, the lime green dragon turned the other way and flew off into the sky, until all that Billy could see of it was a faint green speck. 'Tiresome creature,' said Xing.

'I have to agree with you there,' said Buttons.

'The dragon may have been annoying, but if it is true that soft spots have appeared in the Healing Fields, then we must take care,' said Spark.

'We would have taken care without the warning,' snapped Xing. 'We did not need a dragon talking in circles to tell us about the soft spots.'

'How did that dragon know so much about us?' said Billy.

'Many dragons returned from the Dragon City future. They remember and they talk,' said Spark. 'The dragons who were here, in this realm and this time, heard the stories. And when they realized how the Dragon of Death had been vanquished, most wanted to ensure she, nor any dragon like her, would never rise to power again.'

'And you four set the rules for the new realm – about not swallowing stars or taking power and life force from others,' said Ling-Fei.

'Precisely,' said Buttons. 'And while some may secretly resent us, or yearn for dark magic and power, most want peace.'

'Dragons are not so different to humans then,' said Lola.

'Do not insult us,' said Xing, but Billy heard the smile in her voice. 'That dragon was right about one thing. We're nearly at the Healing Fields.'

'Be careful on our landing,' added Lightning. 'We do not want to land on a soft spot and disappear.'

The Healing Fields

The Healing Fields were not what Billy was expecting.

They were full of flowers ... but that wasn't the strange part. The strange part was that the flowers were enormous. Bigger than trees. Large enough for dragons to land on. Billy felt as if they'd been shrunk and let loose in a garden.

After landing between two huge sunflowers, with stalks so thick Billy couldn't have wrapped his arms around them, they made their way through the forest of flowers. Overhead, huge petals fluttered in the breeze, blocking out light. One fell off and drifted down dangerously close to Dylan's head.

'Careful!' said Charlotte, tugging him out of the way. 'Who knows how much that thing weighs?'

'How come we've never seen the Healing Fields before?' said Billy.

'Our realm is bigger than you can comprehend,' said Spark. 'There is much you have not seen or experienced.'

'And usually Buttons is able to provide the healing that we need,' added Xing, giving the green dragon a sly look. 'But he met his match with the dragobees.'

'Pardon me!' Buttons huffed. 'I'd like to see you try to heal a human child who's been attacked by dragobees! I did my best!'

'And you did a very good job,' said Ling-Fei reassuringly. 'Xing, you need to apologize for teasing Buttons!'

Xing rolled her eyes. 'Fine. I am sorry you could not heal the boy entirely.'

'Xing!' said Ling-Fei.

Xing flashed her teeth in a sharp smile. 'I am sorry that nobody here appreciates my wit.'

Billy couldn't help but laugh. 'I think that's the best apology you're going to get, Buttons.'

'I'll take it,' said Buttons, raising his snout in the air. 'And I'll remember this the next time *you* need healing, Xing.'

Xing cackled in reply and playfully whacked Buttons with her tail.

'The dragobees are no laughing matter,' said Tank, his low voice echoing all around them. 'It is lucky we were close to the Healing Fields. Buttons may have saved the boy's life, but the sooner we find the right plant to fully heal him, the better.'

'How will we know which plant is the right one?' said Billy, staring up at the enormous flowers.

'It will be obvious,' said Spark. 'When we reach the plant we seek, we will take the leaves and wrap Jordan in them. That is what we do for dragons who are injured, and it is what we will do for him.'

Jordan still sat secured to Thunder's back, watching everything happening in silence. Even ever-chatty Midnight had quietened down, but she stayed close to Jordan's side.

'So we've seen tiny dragons; now we're walking through gigantic flowers ... Should I be prepared for a giant ant or something to come crawling out of the earth?' said Lola, stepping carefully around another stalk.

'In this place, you should be prepared for anything,' said Billy.

'What about dinner? Is that going to be prepared anytime soon?' said Lola.

'Glad that somebody asked!' said Dylan. 'Usually I'm the only one who remembers important things such as when it's time to eat.'

Ling-Fei laughed. 'It's true!'

'I don't even know what time it is back home,' said Charlotte, rubbing her eyes. 'I feel as if I've been awake for ten years.'

'Well, it was night when we came through into the Dragon Realm, and it's night again now, so maybe twenty-four hours?' asked Lola.

'Time works differently in our realm,' Spark said. 'And when you travel through a portal, the time does not stay the same as the place where you travelled from.'

Billy frowned. 'So how long have we been gone?'

Spark tilted her head to the side. 'It is difficult to know. When you are at home, I can sense the time there through our bond, and I can sync myself to you. It was how I knew to meet you at your beach at midnight. But if I had to guess, I would say perhaps twelve hours have passed in California since you left.'

'I hope everything is okay back there,' said Billy. 'I mean, how much can go wrong in twelve hours . . . ?'

Ling-Fei wasn't fooled by his false cheer. 'If our theory is right, and things that are disappearing from this realm are appearing in the Human Realm, I think the situation could be very bad back home.'

'She's got a point,' said Lola. She tilted back her head back to gaze up at the top of one of the giant sunflowers. 'Imagine if one of these things popped up unexpectedly in your backyard. Or on the highway.'

'I think an unexpected dragon would be a bigger issue,' said Billy. Especially if it was a dragon who felt less than friendly towards humans, such as the lime green dragon they had seen on their flight here.

'All the more reason for us to find that sword and get back to our world as soon as possible,' said Charlotte firmly. She turned to Buttons. 'Are we close to this healing plant we need to find?'

'There,' said Buttons, pointing with his sharp claws. 'We've found it.'

Billy looked up and gasped. Even if Spark hadn't pointed out which plant it was, Billy would have known this one was special. Like the rest of the plants and flowers in the fields, it was huge, but instead of having green leaves and foliage, it was glowing pale blue. Shimmering blue leaves sprouted at the base and went all the way up the stalk, light flowing throughout it. And at the very top, a dazzlingly brilliant-white flower blossomed, its long slender petals spilling over the top almost like hair.

Ling-Fei ran forward and put her hand on the stalk. 'Oh!' she said, sounding delighted. 'This is a very lovely plant. It's glad to see us!'

'Does she . . . talk to plants?' said Lola. 'I like to garden, but this seems next level.'

'Part of Ling-Fei's power is that she has a deep connection with nature,' explained Charlotte.

'Not just nature. The very earth itself. Once, she convinced a mountain to carry us somewhere,' said Dylan.

'Wow,' said Lola, clearly impressed.

'Ling-Fei, ask if we can take one of its leaves,' instructed Xing.

'Lovely plant,' Ling-Fei said, 'may we take one of your leaves? Our friend is hurt, but we think you can heal him. We are trying to bring peace and stability back to these lands, and we need his help.'

The whole plant trembled, as if it was thinking, and then one of the giant blue leaves gently drifted to the ground.

'Thank you,' said Ling-Fei, both her palms still on the stalk. 'You are a beautiful and generous plant, and I hope you grow for many years to come.'

She stepped away from the healing plant and looked at the others. 'Who knows what to do with this leaf?'

The leaf was the size of a bed sheet. Charlotte and Buttons gently helped Jordan off Thunder's back, and then wrapped him up in the leaf, until he looked like a baby swaddled in a blanket.

'What happens now?' said Billy anxiously. What if the leaf didn't work? What would they do then? Would Jordan be unable to move for ever?

'We wait,' said Spark. 'And hope that it will work.'

'And I'll add my healing power as well.' Buttons began to hum and drum on his belly. 'He'll be well.'

'While we wait, I will find us food, as promised,' said Thunder. 'And when I return, I hope to see that the boy has healed.'

'He will be,' said Midnight fervently. She still hadn't left Jordan's side.

'Be safe,' Lightning said to Thunder. 'I do not like the idea of you going off on your own.'

'I could go with Thunder,' offered Tank.

Thunder shook his head. 'No. You stay in case something unfriendly arrives. I feel more comfortable knowing there are plenty of dragons here.' He turned to Lightning. 'And I am perfectly capable of looking after myself. I know I was bested by those dragobees, but do not doubt me. I can find food for six humans.'

'And for me too!' said Midnight. 'I'm also hungry.'

'I will return with a feast,' said Thunder. 'For all of us.' He looked at the other dragons. 'Be on high alert. If you need to leave this place ...' His voice trailed off.

Billy reached up to his pocket, where the tiny gold flying pig still slept. 'If we do, we'll send you Goldie. She'll take you to wherever we are.'

Thunder nodded. 'A good plan.' Then he spread his enormous wings, careful not to disrupt any of the plants and flowers, and took off into the darkening sky.

The rest of the group moved into the shadow of one of the sunflowers, carrying Jordan with them.

Suddenly his whole body jolted, as if he had been struck by an electric current.

'Ah!' he shouted.

'JORDAN!' cried Midnight, nuzzling his head.

'Midnight, be careful,' said Lightning, and Midnight took a small step back.

'Are you all right?' said Billy, his voice barely concealing his worry.

'I ... I think so? I feel as if I'm getting lightly pinched by hundreds of tiny fingers. It doesn't hurt, but it isn't comfortable.' His eyes lit up. 'I can talk again!'

Lola laughed. 'Yes, it appears so!'

'The healing leaf is pulling the venom out of your body,' said Spark. 'That is what you are feeling.'

'It's kind of like the pins and needles feeling you get when your leg falls asleep,' said Jordan.

'That makes sense,' said Billy with a smile. 'Your whole body has basically been asleep for the past few hours.'

Jordan laughed hoarsely. 'Mate, trust me, I might have been unable to move, but I've been awake. Do you know how terrifying it was to be strapped to a giant dragon BY ITS MOUSTACHE?'

'It seemed like the best idea at the time,' said Billy, but he laughed too. 'I'm glad you're doing better.'

'Me too. And it's thanks to you lot for taking me here to be healed. I know it slowed down your mission.'

'This was more important,' said Ling-Fei.

'We weren't going to leave you frozen by dragobee venom for ever!' added Charlotte.

Jordan cocked an eyebrow. 'So if you didn't need me to find my mum, and the sword, you still would have taken me here?'

'It was lucky for you, and for us, that the two aligned,' said Xing. 'But even I will admit that I am glad we brought you here.'

'Not as glad as me!' said Midnight, bounding forward again. 'Jordan! You *saved* me!'

Jordan slowly sat up and gently patted Midnight.

'And then you saved me! You saved all of us. That was an impressive move you did!'

Midnight ducked her head bashfully. 'Something came over me!'

As Billy watched Jordan and Midnight, he noticed again that Midnight's heart was glowing gold. Just as Spark's had when they'd bonded.

'Midnight!' he burst out. 'Look! I think Jordan is your heart bond human!'

Midnight laughed. 'Of course he is!'

Jordan blinked. 'I am?'

'When you displayed such an act of bravery, of selflessness, it triggered something in Midnight,' said Lightning. 'She too is brave, if a bit rash at times. Your hearts absolutely match. Midnight, I am proud of you.'

Midnight was so excited that she flew up into the air and did a flip. 'This is *the best!*'

The others all laughed and Billy found himself remembering when he had bonded with Spark. It was one of the greatest moments of his life.

'Congratulations,' said Dylan, patting Jordan on the back. 'Your very first, and forever, dragon.'

'Wow,' said Lola, and Billy heard the longing in her voice. 'That's amazing.'

'What happens now?' said Jordan.

'Well, now you have to give Midnight a new name,' said Billy. 'That's part of it, right?'

'Yes, to cement your bond,' said Spark.

Midnight's face fell. 'I . . . I like my name. But I also want a special new heart bond name!'

'I like your name too,' said Jordan slowly. 'How about we add to it?' He tilted his head back and gazed at the pockets of sky visible through the giant sunflower petals. One of the three moons winked above them. 'How about . . . Midnight Moon?'

'I LOVE IT!' shrieked Midnight.

'It's perfect for you,' said Ling-Fei.

'You can still go by Midnight, of course,' said Jordan hurriedly. 'But now you have an official name too.'

'Midnight Moon! Midnight Moon!' sang Midnight. Everyone else laughed and cheered, and Thunder landed at that very moment, bringing fish he'd caught and grilled for their dinner.

As they crowded together, Billy didn't feel afraid.

He was at peace and ready to face whatever came next. They had a new dragon bond on their side and the group was stronger than ever. He glanced up at the sky, his mouth full of fish, and could have sworn that the moon overhead smiled down at them.

Night Flying

Billy was glad that they were all together, and that they now had five heart-bonded humans and dragons. It made him feel as if they could take on anything.

With the new heart bond, Midnight had gone through a transformation. After she'd accepted her new full name of Midnight Moon, her horns had grown even longer, twisting high above her head. And new shining scales, as dark as the midnight sky with flecks of glowing pearl, almost like pieces of the moon itself, had formed all along her back. Her eyes now glowed gold. Billy wondered if they'd had a pearl for Jordan, what power it would have unlocked inside him. Even though Billy had lost his Lightning Pearl back when Spark had given it to the Dragon of Death, he could still feel the power it had given him. It kept growing stronger, even without the pearl being physically present.

When they had eaten their fill of grilled fish, along with peaches they had picked from a nearby grove of peach trees, the group moved deeper into the Healing Fields, finding a sheltered spot beneath one of the giant sunflowers.

'Is it safe here?' said Lightning uneasily. 'We do not want to be pulled into a soft spot.'

'Anywhere is at risk of that,' said Spark gravely.

'What about the floating islands?' said Ling-Fei, gesturing to the sky. 'We slept on one of those before.'

'Even those are not safe,' said Thunder. 'I have witnessed one be pulled into a soft spot, apparently in the sky itself.'

Billy shuddered. Whatever was causing this was extremely powerful.

Lola let out an enormous yawn. 'I don't care where we sleep, as long as we can do it soon. I don't know if I've ever been this tired.'

'Humans,' said Xing, shaking her head. 'If they are not hungry, they are tired.'

'Just wait until you meet an actual baby,' said Dylan. 'They really are always hungry or tired. Trust me, I've been helping with my sisters since they were tiny. Babies are the neediest creatures of any realm.'

'At least they do not talk back,' snapped Xing, but Billy saw the humour in her eyes. 'And we could carry them through the night without having to worry about stopping to rest.'

'But aren't you tired?' asked Jordan. He looked anxiously over at Midnight. 'Especially you, Midnight. You've had a big day.'

'I feel as if I could fly all night!' said Midnight, practically bouncing with energy.

'Dragons don't need as much rest as we do,' Ling-Fei explained. 'Or food. One of the perks of being an ancient, practically immortal, magical beast.'

'Wait,' Billy said, an idea forming. 'The dragons can fly all night.'

'Yes, as we are far superior to you in every way,' said Xing. 'But you apparently need rest.'

Billy kept talking. 'And, Xing, even without us, you can keep seeking the sword, right? Because the magic is so strong?'

'Of course I can. I am a seeker dragon.' Xing paused and sighed dramatically. 'But Ling-Fei's power makes it easier, of course. And I will admit that having the boy to guide us towards his mother also helps. A bond between a mother and son is even stronger than the draw I have towards rare magical items.'

'And the best way to avoid being pulled into a soft spot is to keep flying, right?' Billy went on, his idea crystallizing in his head.

'Again, yes,' said Xing. 'Will you please get to the point? Or are you going to keep asking questions you clearly already know the answer to?'

'We sleep on your backs. The dragons keep flying. Xing uses her power to make sure we're roughly going the right way. When Jordan and Ling-Fei wake up, they can help narrow down what direction we should be going in.'

Billy leaned back on his heels, extremely pleased with himself.

'You want us to function as flying beds?' said Xing flatly.

'I think it is a good idea,' said Spark. 'The children

can get the rest they need, we can avoid soft spots and we will not lose any time.'

'I agree,' said Tank.

'As do I,' said Lightning. 'But my concern is for the human I have been carrying. Your humans can all sleep on you without fear of falling off because of your bond. It is not the same for us.'

'We *could* bond though, couldn't we?' said Lola, a hint of shyness coming into her voice. 'I like you a lot.'

'And I like you as well,' said Lightning gently. 'But the bond is not about that. It is something deeper. Something that cannot be explained.'

'I could do something really brave – protect you the way that Jordan protected Midnight!' said Lola. 'I bet our hearts match.'

'Child, you cannot create a bond just because you wish for one. You do indeed have a good and brave heart. Curious too. But you cannot force your heart to match a dragon's.'

Lola wilted. 'So I'm the loser without a dragon?'

'I can still be your dragon,' said Lightning. 'Just not your heart bond dragon.'

Billy felt a pang for Lola. It must have been hard

to have come along on the adventure but still not feel completely involved. He couldn't imagine what it would be like to be surrounded by dragons, and see the heart bonds at work, but be the only person without one. 'I bet we'll meet your heart bond dragon soon,' he said. 'And you'll know when we do.'

Charlotte also spoke up. 'Don't worry,' she said. 'Right now we have to focus on finding Jordan's mom and that sword, but once everything has calmed down, you can come back to the Dragon Realm with us, and we can find your heart-bonded dragon.' She gave Lola an encouraging smile.

Lola sighed dramatically. 'I suppose I'll just have to be happy with merely flying on a dragon for now.' Then she winked at Lightning. 'I'll take what I can get. But seriously, how am I supposed to stay on your back while I sleep? You remember how tightly I was hanging on!'

Lightning stretched out her long neck. 'I will not soon forget it. You had what I believe is called a "death grip" on me.'

'To avoid falling to my actual death,' said Lola.

'You could ride on Thunder,' suggested Ling-Fei.

'We could tie you to him with his moustache like we did with Jordan.'

'That worked for a short distance,' said Thunder. 'But I do not know how long my moustache can be used as a harness.'

'I can also confirm it's extremely uncomfortable,' said Jordan. 'No offence. Obviously, I'm really grateful.'

'It's the right idea though,' said Billy as he glanced around the Healing Fields. 'There has to be some kind of vine or something here that we can use to secure you to Lightning.'

'I like the sound of that more than being secured by a moustache, but what if the vine gets loose somehow? And I don't notice because I'm asleep?'

'I will notice,' said Lightning. 'And if you fall, I will catch you.'

'I will fly at a slightly lower elevation than everyone else,' said Thunder. 'That way, if you slip, I will see right away.'

'You can trust us to keep you safe,' said Spark. 'None of us are your heart bond dragon, but we will take care of you.'

'Do not make promises you cannot keep,' said Xing roughly. 'Yes, we will try our best, but these are dangerous and unpredictable times. We cannot promise to keep anyone safe. As much as we would like to.'

'Is that supposed to be reassuring?' said Lola.

'That's about as reassuring as Xing gets,' said Ling-Fei. 'But if it helps, I trust the dragons. You won't fall.'

'Well, I definitely don't want to hold the group back.' Lola grinned at everyone. 'Find a vine and tie me up!'

Billy hadn't been sure he would actually be able to fall asleep on Spark, despite it being his idea that they fly through the night. But once they were all back in the sky, with Lola securely fastened to Lightning with not one but several vines, he felt his eyes grow heavy.

Sleep, Billy, Spark said down their bond. *You will need your rest for what is to come.*

Something in her words snapped him wide awake. *Have you seen something?* he asked. *I mean, see as in see the future?* As a seer dragon, Spark had visions of the future. Because of their bond, sometimes Billy even saw her visions in his dreams.

Everything I have seen is shifting. The visions are blurry. I have seen a great clock, and I believe I have seen the same sea dragon you saw at the beach. I have also seen the sword. Sometimes it is in the hands of a woman who looks like Jordan, sometimes in the hands of a man with a face I cannot make out. I have seen a rock, again and again, but I do not know what it means.

Should we tell the others? Billy didn't want to keep anything from them, especially if it was important.

There is nothing to tell, only fleeting images. But even without my visions, I know that you need your rest. We face a great unknown, but whatever it is, it is powerful. You will want to be at your strongest.

Billy knew she was right, and even though he was certain they were heading into unknown danger, he felt safe on Spark. Her presence always reassured him. So he closed his eyes and leaned his head against the back of Spark's neck, letting the steady rhythm of her flying lull him to sleep.

'Billy. Billy, wake up!'

Billy felt a sharp jab in his side and his eyes flew

open. For a moment, he was completely disoriented. Where was he? Was he moving?

Everything came rushing back to him. He was on Spark. He'd fallen asleep on her back. The sun was just starting to rise, turning the sky into a brilliant tapestry of purple and pink.

Ling-Fei's face popped into Billy's view, her black braids dangling down and tickling his nostrils. Billy swatted Ling-Fei's hair out of his face and then laughed. She was hanging upside down from Xing, who was flying over Spark.

'You're a deep sleeper,' said Ling-Fei. 'Even when you're sleeping on a dragon!'

'Is something happening? Why did you wake me up?'

Ling-Fei swung back around on Xing's back, and Xing lowered herself so she was flying next to Spark.

'I can't believe you let Ling-Fei do that,' Billy grumbled at Spark.

'It seemed a good way to wake you,' said Spark.

'Is everyone awake?' Billy glanced over and saw Lola slumped on Lightning's back, apparently snoring. But Jordan had woken up and was sitting straight up on Midnight, his eyes focused on the horizon ahead.

'We're close,' said Ling-Fei simply.

'How do you know?'

'I feel something ... strange. Something ... powerful.'

Billy sat up a little straighter.

'It's hard to explain, but ever since we've been back in the Dragon Realm, my power with nature has become stronger. There's so much chaotic energy everywhere right now. It's as if I've had a constant ringing in my ears that's been getting louder and louder until it's almost all I can hear. But something has changed. When I woke up, everything was quiet again. Except for that direction.' Ling-Fei pointed towards the rising sun. 'I feel as if whatever is causing all of this disruption is that way. And I'm even more certain that it's linked to the sword.'

Billy realized that his agility skill also seemed to be coming back, even without the Lightning Pearl. He remembered how just before he'd fallen asleep the night before, he had caught a gnat between his fingers that had been buzzing near his ear. And he'd even managed to be so precise that the gnat had flown away unharmed when he'd let go.

'I too feel a draw in that direction,' said Xing. 'That is why we have been flying that way all night.' The morning light danced on her silver scales.

'It is possible that Jordan's mother is attempting to return the sword to where it came from, which means she is close to a great power source,' added Spark.

'The Forbidden Fountain?' asked Billy, remembering what Tank had said the day before.

'No, the Forbidden Fountain is where the sword was formed, but not where it was hidden,' said Tank. 'Once you take something from the Forbidden Fountain, you cannot return it. This is another powerful source.' He had flown closer to them during the conversation. Charlotte still slept on his back. Buttons flew up on Billy's other side, along with a yawning Dylan.

'Is it possible that the sword was hidden in the In-Between?' said Spark. 'And that is where Jordan's mother is trying to get to?'

'The In-Between?' asked Dylan as he stretched. He glanced down at the ground beneath them. 'I have to say, I do *not* like waking up this high in the air.'

'The Human and Dragon Realms don't sit

directly next to each other. There's a space called the In-Between holding them together,' explained Buttons. He tilted his head to the side with a thoughtful expression. 'There's so much unbalance in our realm right now, and it's spreading into the Human Realm. The rules of our world, of what belongs here and what belongs in the Human Realm, seem to be changing. I wonder if the In-Between has something to do with it. Especially if humans are now somehow aware of it.'

'Even dragons do not know how to get into the In-Between,' said Lightning. 'It is a hidden place. If that is indeed where Jordan's mother is going, it will be almost impossible to find her.'

'Humans do not know about the In-Between,' scoffed Xing.

'Humans are also not meant to know about the Dragon Realm, and yet it sounds as if Jordan's mother not only knows about this realm, but she knows how to get here. I do not think we should underestimate her,' said Tank.

Jordan suddenly looked over. 'I think she's close! I can't explain how I know, but I can feel it.'

'Midnight, fly up here with me,' ordered Xing. 'You and Jordan will guide the way.'

They cut through the morning sky, urgency driving them forward. Billy kept an eye out for soft spots, hoping if he saw any that they might give him a clue to help figure out what was happening between the realms.

Today, they didn't see any other dragons as they flew, which felt strange. Billy realized they hadn't seen any since they'd passed the hostile lime green dragon.

Do you know where we are? Billy asked Spark through their bond. While most of the Dragon Realm was lush and green, they had entered a part of the realm that Billy could only describe as a desert. He wasn't sure if it was because the landscape had all disappeared into a soft spot, or if it was, in fact, sandy wasteland in the realm.

Something has happened here. This land should not look this way. We are flying over what should be one of our great seas, Spark thought back.

Ahead of Billy, Ling-Fei suddenly sat bolt upright.

'We're close!' she said. 'To something big. I can feel it!'

In the distance, Billy thought he could make out a large rock formation. It was the only thing in sight for miles. 'Do you guys see that up ahead?' He remembered what Spark had said about seeing a rock in her visions. Was this that rock?

'You mean the big rock tower that's jutting up in the middle of nowhere?' said Lola, who had woken up when the dragons had increased their pace. She was no longer tied to Lightning and looked much more comfortable today than she had yesterday.

Charlotte leaned forward. 'I think I can see something at the base of that big rock.'

'Not something – someone!' said Jordan breathlessly. 'That's a person!'

'Stay together, in formation,' said Thunder. 'No matter what.'

As they flew closer and closer, Billy saw that Jordan was right. There was a hunched figure at the base of the rock, and this person was holding a long, large object that glinted in the light.

'I think that's my mum!' Jordan yelled. 'Mum! It's me, Jordan!'

If the figure could hear Jordan, they didn't take any notice.

'Go faster, Midnight! Faster!' yelled Jordan, as the group raced towards the rock. When they were closer, Billy saw that the rock stood in a shallow pool of water that reflected the sky, creating a strange mirage effect.

'Be prepared to fight,' said Thunder.

'That's my mum!' said Jordan again. 'She's good – she's on our side!'

'We still do not know who that is. And we should be cautious,' said Lightning. 'Even if it is your mother, there might be others with her.'

'I'm not fighting my mum! I'm here to save her!' said Jordan.

Billy kept a close eye on the figure, trying to determine if Jordan was right. He could hardly make out if it was even a person, much less anything that would let Jordan identify the figure as his mom. But he remembered what Xing had said, about the pull between a mother and child. If Jordan said that was his mom, it probably was.

The figure was waving a long, shimmering object back and forth in the air. Then they lifted it over their head and sliced it down in front of them, directly into the rock itself. The rock crackled with power for a brief moment and, as it did, the figure seemed to step directly into it and vanish into thin air.

The Riddle and the Rock

'MUM!' Jordan shouted, his voice breaking. But there was nobody there.

'Be careful when we land,' called out Spark. 'We do not know what that rock is capable of.'

As the group landed at the base of the rock, Billy realized that the water was only a few centimetres deep. Spark landed with a small splash, sending ripples out in all directions. Billy jumped off Spark and stared at the rock, trying to figure out how the figure had disappeared into it. He walked around the rock formation, careful not to get too close, looking for any cracks in its exterior, or for any secret passages. The rock was smooth all over like a pebble at the bottom of a stream.

'Is this some sort of magic rock?' asked Lola as she hopped off Lightning. 'Like another one of those portals that we jumped through?' She frowned. 'This looks like a pretty normal rock to me.'

'Trust me, looks can be deceiving,' said Dylan. 'Once I got stuck inside a tree.'

'I forgot about that,' said Charlotte, stifling a laugh.

'It isn't something you forget when it happens to you,' grumbled Dylan. 'But I'm glad someone can laugh about it.'

Charlotte grinned at him. 'I'm only laughing because you were totally fine! But it was pretty funny when we heard the tree talk with your voice.'

'Guys, focus,' said Billy. 'We need to figure this out.'

'Actually,' said Ling-Fei, 'that's just given me an idea. Maybe Jordan's mom is now trapped in the rock, like Dylan was trapped in the tree! We all saw her go into it, right?' She raised her voice. 'Hello! Jordan's mom! Can you hear us?'

The rock stayed silent.

'This is ridiculous!' said Jordan. 'We have to *do* something! Shouting at rocks won't help. We have to get to my mum! Maybe she got sucked into a soft spot?'

'I don't think so,' said Ling-Fei. 'If it were a soft spot, the rock would have been sucked in too.'

'Then how did she just disappear?'

'I think your mother has indeed found an entrance into the In-Between,' said Spark solemnly.

'How can that be?' said Xing, a hint of awe in her voice. 'Even *we* have never been to the In-Between.'

'I believe I have seen it in a vision,' said Spark. 'I did not realize until now that it was Jordan's mother who was at the centre of the vision, but it is clear to me that she has somehow found a way there.'

'I know Buttons said the In-Between is a place between the two realms, but how can someone *go* there?' said Billy, his brow furrowing in confusion.

Dylan pushed his glasses up on his nose. 'I'm still pretty confused about what exactly the In-Between is.'

'I will do my best to explain.' Spark breathed out a stream of frost that covered the base of the rock and formed pictures that danced around like firelight. 'As you now know, our worlds are separated into two realms – the Dragon Realm and the Human Realm. But between the two realms, there are pockets that exist. Pockets that you can travel to that hold some of the most magical properties in all the lands. Imagine that our realms are held together by a powerful magic, but the seal is not perfect. There are areas where the magic has pooled and bulged and created a pocket that you can visit. These magical pockets between our realms are few and far between, but they exist and we refer to them simply as the In-Between. We believe that when the sword was hidden, it was placed in one of these pockets in the In-Between as it does not belong to either realm and would be almost impossible to find.'

'But how would a human get into the In-Between?' mused Lightning. 'Dragons do not know how to reach it, let alone humans.'

'Jordan's mom was waving something around before she disappeared,' said Billy. 'Maybe the sword is how she got in? It can cut through *anything*, right?'

'Perhaps,' said Thunder, looking thoughtful.

'It is a good theory,' said Spark. 'I have never seen the sword with my own eyes, but I have seen it in visions. I will try to recreate it for you all. Perhaps you will see something I have missed.' She blew out another cloud of cold air, except this time it began to solidify, forming an ice sculpture. The ice took the shape of a sword with two wings forming the hilt at the base of the sword and a large jewel set between the wings. Engravings of humans and dragons covered the length of the blade, which sparkled as if it were cut from diamond.

Lola let out a gasp. 'Woah. That is a cool sword. Is that the sword that your mom had, Jordan?'

Jordan scratched his head. 'The one I saw didn't have any of those engravings, and it definitely didn't sparkle like that.'

'The blade is said to be made of the hardest stone known to either realm and it is completely transparent,' said Xing.

'Well, the one I saw was really big like this one, but it was pretty dull and it *definitely* didn't sparkle,' Jordan said. He paused for a moment. 'But now that I'm thinking about it, the sword was sheathed when I saw it . . .'

Dylan stood up on his toes to take a closer look at the ice sword. 'I'm guessing this ice sword doesn't work as well as the real thing.'

Billy tried to put all the pieces together in his head.

He stared at the sword – at the intricate images all along the side.

'Is that . . . writing?' he said, stepping closer.

Ling-Fei's eyes lit up. 'Maybe it's a clue!'

'It is written in the old dragon language,' said Tank. He gazed at Spark. 'How were you able to recreate it in such detail?'

'I have seen it many times, in many visions,' said Spark. Then she looked away. 'And the Dragon of Death was obsessed with finding it. She had replicas of it in the Tower. They matched the sword I had seen in my visions, so I knew what it was. It is as if the image of the sword has been burned onto my mind, even though I have never seen it with my own eyes.'

'What's written on the side of the sword?' asked Charlotte.

'On one side there appears to be a warning of some kind,' said Spark. 'Hinting at the sword's power, and what might happen if it falls into the wrong hands. Let me read it in the old dragon language first, and then I will try to translate.' Spark's eyes glowed gold as she read the script on the side of the sword, and her voice came out in a way Billy had never heard.

Some sounds were lilting, like a song, and some were low and rough and little more than growls. He felt as though he was in a trance, as if Spark were casting a spell.

After she finished, she spoke each line again, this time in English.

> 'Before you pick me up, take care;
> What I cut, you can never repair.
> For I can slice a star from the sky
> As easy as I can cut out your eye.
> Nothing can stop me, no sword nor shield;
> What I cut can never be healed.
> The more I cut, the sharper I grow;
> Fill me with light, not blood, and I will glow.
> Wield me carefully, slice and saw;
> I do not belong to man nor dragon claw.
> And if you take me, you should atone,
> For the rock alone is my home.'

Charlotte let out a low whistle. 'Well, that's a warning if ever I heard one. Who would use the sword after reading that?'

'But presumably only dragons can understand what it says,' said Dylan.

'I bet my mum would be able to read it,' said Jordan. 'She's studied all kinds of ancient languages. I wouldn't be surprised if she could read an ancient dragon tongue.'

'Interesting,' said Tank.

'So we know that the sword wants to stay put, but if you're going to use it, you'd better watch out,' said Lola, ticking things off on her fingers. 'And it likes light more than blood, whatever that means.'

'Strange, since it's literally called the Blood Sword,' said Dylan.

'And did you hear the part about the rock?' added Ling-Fei. 'It says the rock is its home.'

They all stared at the giant rock in front of them.

'See – I told you my mum was a good guy!' said Jordan. 'She's obviously putting the sword back where it belongs.'

'So it would seem,' said Xing. 'But we cannot assume. We must figure out how to follow her into the In-Between.'

'What does it say on the other side?' asked Billy. 'Maybe that will give us another clue.'

Spark cleared her throat and spoke again in the same strange language. When she translated this side, it was a little shorter.

'Buried deep and buried dark;
You have one chance to make your mark.
My bed is hidden in this rock;
Only one way to unlock.
Thunder wills the ground to shake
As lightning wills me to wake
When it flashes across the sky,
Know it is your time to try.
Remember I am not to keep;
I would rather be fast asleep.'

'Thunder and Lightning!' squealed Midnight, who'd been surprisingly quiet since they'd landed. 'That must mean my parents can help!'

'It's *quite* the coincidence,' said Dylan.

'Y'all know I don't believe in coincidences,' said Charlotte. 'But it is handy that we've got a dragon who can bring on thunder and *two* who can summon lightning.' She looked at Spark's crackling gold antlers pointedly. 'Didn't you hear? "Lightning wills me to wake". Well, let's wake that thing up!'

Everyone stared at her.

Charlotte sighed dramatically. 'Isn't it obvious? You strike the rock with lightning to open it to get to the sword.'

'But the riddle is on the sword, not on the rock,' said Dylan, frowning.

'Well, they can't totally spell it out otherwise anyone passing by this rock could realize what to do,' said Charlotte. 'The riddle only works if you know what you're looking for, and we know we're looking for the sword. Plus, it literally says, "My bed is hidden in this rock" – the sword is telling us where to find it.'

Spark blinked. 'I never thought of it like that.'

'The result may just be a rock sliced in two,' said Tank.

'Or it could open it,' said Billy. 'It's worth a shot, and we don't have any better ideas. Plus, we're running out of time.' He glanced over at Jordan, who was still staring at the rock where his mother had disappeared with a stricken expression on his face. Billy knew he must be terrified for his mom. But more than that,

Billy knew they had to make sure the sword was back where it belonged. And that it stayed there. The riddles on the sword had only made him more anxious about it. Clearly, it was meant to be left alone.

'If we're going to strike the rock with lightning, may I tell it first?' said Ling-Fei. 'It doesn't sound like a very pleasant experience.'

'Be careful,' warned Xing. 'I would rather you stay on my back while you touch the rock, just in case.'

Xing flew close to the rock and Ling-Fei rested her hands on it. Billy held his breath, waiting for something terrible to happen. But nothing did. He exhaled and tried to calm his pounding heart.

'Rock,' Ling-Fei said politely. 'We're going to strike you with lightning, because we think there is something inside you that we need to find.'

She waited a moment and then nodded, as if she had been answered. 'I don't think the rock will mind.'

'Well, now that we've been polite about it, can we go ahead and get some lightning going?' said Charlotte. 'Who knows what could be happening in there?'

Everyone looked at Lightning and Spark. The two

dragons, who both had the power to control lightning and electricity, nodded at each other.

'On your count,' said Lightning.

'Everyone, back up,' added Spark. 'One, two, three!'

Huge bolts of lightning shot out of her horns at the same time as Lightning blasted her own crackling strikes at the rock. As they struck the surface, the water all around the rock began to shimmer and steam.

'Quick! Children! Out of the water!' cried Buttons. 'Climb onto our backs!' Careful not to touch Spark's still crackling antlers, Billy leaped on. Then he saw that Lola was still standing, frozen with panic as the water continued to bubble.

'Lola!' he shouted desperately. He couldn't lead Spark to her – she was too busy sending bolts of lightning at the rock – but then Charlotte grabbed Lola's hand and yanked her up onto Tank.

Lola blinked. 'Oh my goodness, I'm so sorry. I don't know what happened! Everything moved so fast and suddenly there were lightning bolts, and I didn't know how to get on Lightning without getting struck and . . .'

'Don't worry,' said Charlotte. 'We've got you. You're part of our team now.'

Spark and Lightning continued their lightning power blasts, and then a bolt from each dragon struck exactly in the middle, before ricocheting back up towards the sky and boomeranging back to the rock. As the lightning blast hit the rock, it began to crackle and shimmer, and with a mighty groan, it cleaved in two.

But instead of being able to see beyond it, to the sky of the Dragon Realm, they were looking *into* it.

Charlotte had been right.

An inky darkness with glittering lights, like tiny stars, beckoned. It looked like the night sky.

Very slowly, the rock began to close, and Billy realized they had to move fast.

'Quick!' he cried. 'Everyone in! Stay together!'

The group burst through the opening at once and before they even knew it, they were in a brand new realm.

The In-Between.

The In-Between

The rock slammed shut with a thunderous crack. Billy blinked, trying to get his bearings. It was dim, with no natural light appearing from anywhere. The swirling darkness all around them was dotted with glittering light, but it was still hard to make out his surroundings. As Billy's eyes adjusted, he saw that they were on what appeared to be a long, winding stone bridge, with a sparkling body of water on either side. The bridge looked as if it was a dragon's back surfacing out of a magic lake, splitting it in two. Above them, a dense, dark fog blanketed the air, making it difficult to fly. Thick roots hung down from the fog like ropes. This felt like a place that was wedged between worlds, Billy thought to himself.

'MUM!' Jordan yelled, unable to contain himself. 'MUM, are you here?'

'*Jordan?*' said a voice up ahead. A silhouette of a tall, slender woman with curly hair appeared from the stone bridge. 'Jordan, what are you doing here?' She took a step back as Jordan came into her view. 'And are you riding a *dragon*? Oh my! This can't be real.' She rubbed her eyes.

'Mum, it is real. I'm here!'

'But . . . how? You shouldn't be here! How did you find a dragon? And other children?' Jordan's mom was so stunned that she gripped the edge of the stone bridge as if she might fall off if she let go. 'Are you okay?'

Jordan rolled his eyes. 'I'm *fine*, Mum. I followed you into the portal, and luckily I found these guys, who helped me find you. But I should be asking you the same thing. What are you doing with a dangerous, magic sword?'

Billy could see the long sword sheathed and strapped to her back.

'I'm trying to right a wrong,' said Jordan's mom firmly.

Before she could say more, there was a flash of silver, and Jordan's mom cried out, 'Give me my sword back! I need to return it!'

Xing floated back towards the group, the *sanguinem gladio* hanging on a leather strap from her sharp teeth. 'Unfortunately, we do not have time for these ... pleasantries.' She glared at Jordan's mom, her eyes a smouldering gold. 'This is not *your* sword. It does not belong to anyone. It must be you who has caused all the chaos between the realms. And if there is anything that should be given to you, it is a kick to push you off this stone bridge to trap you in the eternal emptiness of the rivers that flow beside us now.'

Midnight burst forward into the space between Xing and Jordan's mom.

'You stay away from my mum!' Jordan cried. 'She might have the sword, but she's obviously trying to help.' He paused and looked back at his mom. 'Right, Mum?'

Jordan's mom held out her hands in front of her. 'Listen, I know how this looks. But I promise you, I'm on your side. I'm trying to fix a wrong that I'll admit I enabled. I'm a scientist. And I've been helping the TURBO company with research. I helped my boss, Frank Albert, find this sword, and I'm ashamed to admit that I also helped him find the Forbidden Fountain.'

The dragons gasped. 'It can be found?'

Jordan's mom nodded and looked away with shame. 'He's been cutting holes between the realms to find it. I told him to stop, that we didn't know the repercussions, but he was like a man possessed. And then, he finally found it – the Forbidden Fountain – and he brought back some of the golden elixir for us to use in his labs. But then, one day last week, I went to ask him a question, and I caught him using the elixir on himself with some sort of invention I'd never seen before. And I realized then that it had never been about the research. It was because he was desperate for power.'

Spark let out a gasp.

'I know!' said Jordan's mom. 'That was my exact reaction. So I stole the sword back and now I'm returning it to its place between the realms. I can't return the golden elixir to the Forbidden Fountain, but once the sword is locked back in this rock, Frank won't be able to find it. I found it the first time, and I brought it to him. Once it's where it belongs, he'll never find it on his own. And, as I'm sure you know, the Forbidden Fountain is never in the same place, so without the sword, that will be lost to Frank too.'

Xing still looked suspicious.

'I think we can trust Jordan's mom,' said Ling-Fei.

'Of course we can trust her!' said Jordan.

'We do not have time to waste,' said Thunder. 'Where does the sword live?'

'Follow me.'

Jordan's mom turned on her heels and raced down the bridge. The dragons and the children on their backs followed until the path abruptly came to an end. Billy wasn't sure what he expected the sword's home to look like. Perhaps a stone with a sword-shaped hole in it. Or an ornate sheath in special housing. But he was expecting *something*. He looked around to see what he was missing. Was there something hidden in the shadows? But all he could see was the end of the path that finished on a cliff edge.

'Is this where the sword goes, er . . . Jordan's mom?' Billy asked.

Jordan's mom smiled. 'You can call me Professor Edwards. And, yes, this is where the sword is kept.' She took a pin from her pocket and quickly pricked her finger before squeezing a drop of blood onto the ground at the end of the path. She looked back at Billy and gave him a wink. 'Sometimes there's more than meets the eye.' The ground shook for a moment before rising up, leaving an indentation in the shape of the *sanguinem gladio*. 'See,' said Professor Edwards, gesturing at the indentation in the ground. 'Do you believe me now?'

Xing grumbled. 'It appears you are telling the truth. Take the sword and return it to its home.' With a flick of her head, Xing tossed the sword towards Professor Edwards.

But before she could say more, the whole In-Between lit up with electricity. Jordan's mom stared at the ceiling in horror. 'Oh, no!' she said, panic making her voice rise. 'Frank's coming! He must have worked out how to use the TURBO lightning generator to open the rock!'

A loud *crack* sounded above them, and Billy looked up to see a white man with short blond hair appear out of the fog above them. He was flying in a hovercraft of sorts, his arm pointed at the sword. A flash of light shot out of his outstretched hand like a lasso, wrapping around the sword.

'No!' shouted Professor Edwards, desperately reaching for the sword.

'Give it back!' shouted Billy, fear twisting his stomach into knots.

Spark shot out a burst of electricity at the intruder, but the hovercraft dodged out of the way.

Frank caught the sword in his hands and revealed a wide, toothy smile. 'That was very naughty of you, Professor Edwards, to steal my sword. But luckily I put a tracker in it, so I was able to follow you here. And, of course, you'd already translated the riddle for me, so I knew how to enter the rock.' Then he grinned at the sword. 'But now I can go anywhere I want, thanks to this beauty.'

Before anyone could react, Frank slashed the sword through the air in front of him, creating a portal. He zipped through it, leaving nothing but fog behind him.

Always a Hatchling

'He's gone!' Billy reached out to where Frank had disappeared, his hands grasping at empty air. 'Where did he go? How did he do that with his hands?' He turned to Professor Edwards. 'Does he have magical powers?'

Professor Edwards looked pained. 'I don't know what happens when a human uses the golden elixir, but it appears Frank has gained enhanced powers. And he clearly used it on the TURBO prototypes.'

'Is that how the dude was flying around on a hovercraft, shooting laser lassos out of his hands?' said Lola.

Professor Edwards let out a sharp laugh and

nodded. 'Yes, the hovercraft is a TURBO prototype, and he's wearing a high-tech mechanical device over his arm called an Infinite Laser Arm that can do all sorts of things, even before the addition of the golden elixir. It's meant to be used for surgeries requiring high levels of precision, but apparently he's using it to steal swords that don't belong to him.'

'Now we know what has been causing the soft spots and making everything so unstable,' said Spark solemnly.

'Yes, it must be all the holes he's been cutting between the realms in his search for the Forbidden Fountain,' replied Buttons.

Ling-Fei's brow furrowed. 'So Frank has been to all the places in the Dragon Realm where things have been disappearing?'

Xing shook her head. 'Not exactly. By taking the *sanguinem gladio* from where it is meant to be hidden, and cutting holes between our realms, he has weakened the entire In-Between, which has made everything more unstable. My theory is that it is causing the Dragon Realm to collapse on top of the Human Realm.'

'Are the holes the same as portals?' asked Dylan.

'Portals are much more stable. They can be closed and controlled. But while it seems that the holes can be used as a type of portal between the realms, they're not the same,' explained Buttons.

'So when we find Frank, get the sword back and return it to its place, everything will go back to normal, right?' said Billy as he tried to ignore how his palms were starting to sweat.

'You heard what was written on the sword,' said Lightning. 'The cuts cannot be mended. The holes between our realms cannot be closed. And the parts of Dragon Realm that have already appeared in the Human Realm may be in your realm for ever.'

'For ever?' squeaked Lola.

'We are still unsure about what exactly has disappeared in our realm and what now exists in the Human Realm,' said Spark. 'We must get to your realm as soon as possible. To find Frank, and to see what is happening there.'

'Frank will have gone back to London,' said Professor Edwards. 'He'll have taken the sword to the TURBO headquarters.'

'Then London is where we will go,' said Thunder.

'What about California?' said Lola, tugging on her hair. It was the most nervous Billy had ever seen her. 'We know things are happening there too. That's where we saw the sea dragon, and that's where . . . my mom is.' She glanced over at Professor Edwards and Jordan. 'I'm worried about her, and she'll be worried about me. I didn't even leave a note.'

Billy took a deep breath and made a decision. 'I promise we'll go to California when this is all figured out, but we have to go to London first. If Frank Albert gets any more powerful, our families will be in even more danger.'

Lola's face fell, but then she rolled her shoulders back and seemed to steel herself. 'Okay.'

'I'm sorry that I dragged you into this mess,' said Billy.

'Well, technically I made you take me with you,' said Lola.

'Lola,' said Lightning gently. 'I can always try to take you back to your home. With things being so unstable, it is much easier now to create portals.'

Lola shook her head. 'No, I said I wanted to help

and I meant it. I know I don't have superpowers, or even a dragon bond, but I want to do something. I feel as if I need to be here. With all of you.' She flushed. 'I know that sounds silly – to make such a huge choice based on a feeling.'

'Not at all,' said Spark. 'Your instincts are powerful. You should trust them. And in my visions, I have seen you with us in London, Lola. It is hazy, but you are there. I see us all together, and I see a tower with a clock. I think you are right – you are meant to stay.'

'I agree,' said Billy with a smile. 'I'm glad you're here with us.'

'Me too,' said Charlotte.

'We clearly need all the help we can get,' added Dylan.

'Then it is decided,' said Thunder. 'We will all go to London.' He raised a giant furry brow. 'I have never been to a city run by humans. The only city I have ever known is Dragon City.'

'Well,' said Billy, 'I've never been to London, but I'm sure it's very different to Dragon City.'

'Looks as if I'll be the one showing you around this time,' said Jordan, grinning broadly. 'We probably won't have time for a bus tour, but I'll point out the major sights from the sky.'

'Jordan! You will do no such thing. You will go straight home, lock the doors and stay there,' said Professor Edwards. 'And I'll go to the TURBO office to deal with Frank.'

'No disrespect meant, Mum, but I've got a dragon now. These guys need me. Didn't you just hear Dylan? They need all the help they can get.' Jordan looked at Billy and the others for confirmation.

Billy nodded. 'It's true. We do need him.'

Professor Edwards pinched the bridge of her nose. 'Jordan, you know I can't allow you to do this.'

'Mum, I'm doing it with or without your permission,' said Jordan. 'I have to help.'

'It is hard when your children take flight,' said Lightning as she glanced lovingly at Midnight. 'But at some point, you have to let them fly. Billy and Jordan are right – we will need all the help we can get in the battle ahead of us. You can help by telling us everything you know about Frank and the TURBO organization. And Jordan can help by flying by our side. He is ready for this.'

Professor Edwards's eyes shone and she blinked back tears. 'I just want to protect my son.'

'I know,' said Lightning. 'They will always be hatchlings to us.'

'I am not a hatchling!' cried Midnight in indignation.

'Me neither!' exclaimed Jordan. 'I'm the one who followed you into the Dragon Realm to come to your rescue! Lightning is right. I can do this.'

Professor Edwards nodded. 'I believe in you, Jordan, and I'm so proud of you. But as Lightning said, you'll always be my hatchling.'

'*Mum!* Stop getting so mushy! We have bigger things to concentrate on, like finding your terrible boss and then saving the world.'

'You can ride with me,' said Thunder to Professor Edwards. 'But hang on tight.' Everyone climbed onto their respective dragons.

'To London,' said Spark, and together with the other dragons, she opened a swirling portal in the In-Between.

'Goodness,' breathed Professor Edwards. 'This is the most incredible portal I have ever seen. I wish I had time to study it more closely . . .'

'Well, you're about to get very close to it. On the count of three, everybody in!' Billy said, feeling the familiar buzz of adrenaline rush through him as they prepared to jump. He knew that they were leaping into the unknown, but they were together. And they were going to fix this. He was sure of it.

Then as one, the group of dragons and their riders leaped into the crackling and swirling portal, leaving the shining rivers of the In-Between behind.

London Bridge Is Falling Down

The River Thames was on fire.

And there was a dragon sitting on top of Tower Bridge.

After all he'd seen and experienced, Billy didn't think anything could shock him, but when they came barrelling out of the portal that the dragons had made in the In-Between and into the sky above London, his jaw dropped.

There were dragons *everywhere*. There was the one on Tower Bridge, two on St Paul's Cathedral, four circling the Houses of Parliament and even more in the sky. They were diving, dodging and breathing great streams of fire.

'Oh my goodness,' said Professor Edwards, her voice trembling. 'Things have ... escalated quickly.'

As Billy tried to make sense of what he was seeing, there was a mighty *boom* and, as if by magic, an island appeared in the sky. Billy knew instantly that it was a floating island from the Dragon Realm.

People on the riverbanks who had been running and screaming now stopped to stare wide-eyed at the island hovering in mid-air. And then, as if the island suddenly realized that gravity worked differently in the Human Realm than in the Dragon Realm, it shook free from its place in the sky and dropped towards the earth like an asteroid.

'Run!' yelled someone from below, just before the island crashed into the River Thames.

Billy's vision blurred. He couldn't believe what he was seeing. As terrifying as the Dragon Realm had been this past summer, Billy always took comfort in the fact that it was a world away – an almost mythical place that only Billy and his friends knew about. But now, his worlds were colliding, and Billy wasn't sure if the earth would ever be the same again.

The sound of buzzing helicopters and thundering

roars snapped Billy from his thoughts. He realized his worlds weren't just colliding; they were at war. There was another loud *boom* as what looked like an electric net was fired out from one of the helicopters. Although it looked like a net, it didn't move like one. It zigzagged through the sky, flickering in and out of sight, like a moving picture in a misaligned flipbook. At first, Billy couldn't make out which direction the net was travelling in, but then he realized it wasn't moving on a straight path – it was chasing a fleeing dragon. The dragon dipped and dived, desperately trying to get away, but each time the net flickered back into sight, it was closer to the dragon.

'What is that contraption that these humans are shooting out of their flying machines?' said Thunder, his deep voice unsteady.

'Surely it is a wasted effort,' Xing hissed. 'No human-made net can contain a dragon.'

'I know dragons are meant to be really smart,' said Lola, eyes glued to the net flashing through the sky, 'but do you *see* that thing? It's disappearing and reappearing in the air like a heat-seeking strobe light! That *definitely* isn't a normal net.'

'You're right, Lola,' said Professor Edwards. 'That net must be made by TURBO.' She paused and took a sharp breath. 'I knew Frank and his teams had been using materials from the Dragon Realm to experiment with new products, but I've never seen this before. All the projects I was aware of were still very early prototypes. Nothing was even close to being used in real life.'

The net flashed closer and closer until ... *snap*. It wrapped itself around the dragon, pinning its wings to its body, and dropped into the River Thames below, the dragon thrashing inside it.

Boom. Boom. Boom.

'Look out!' roared Tank. 'They have fired nets at us!'

Billy's breath caught in his throat as he saw three flashing nets zigzagging towards them at an impossible speed.

'We have to do something!' Jordan said.

'Blast those nets!' Charlotte yelled, and Tank puffed up his chest and hurled a giant fireball at them. But the nets dodged the attack with ease, flickering out of sight just before the fireball struck, before reappearing even closer than ever.

Xing, Spark and Lightning fired a barrage of ice and electricity at the nets, but their attacks were just as easily avoided.

Dylan covered his eyes. 'I really hope these nets aren't painful.'

'We're not going to find out if I can help it,' said Ling-Fei as she zoomed to the front of the group on Xing. 'I'm hoping I still have enough of my power to control the wind.' She gave Xing a gentle pat on her back. 'Give me strength through our bond.' Ling-Fei closed her eyes and clasped her hands together. Nothing happened at first, but after a moment, the air around them began to swirl. Her eyes shot open and the wind swirled faster and faster, until finally, she pushed her hands out in front of her, creating a column of wind so powerful that Billy could see it in the air.

The nets flickered, shifting back and forth as if trying to escape, but each time they flashed back into sight, they were a little further away.

'It's working!' said Lola. 'Ling-Fei, you're doing it!'

'I don't know how long I can hold this for,' said Ling-Fei, her face scrunched in effort.

As she spoke, Billy could see the blast of wind was weakening and the nets were now creeping closer again.

Ling-Fei's arms were shaking. 'I . . . I . . . can't hold it any longer.' And with a *whoosh*, the column of wind disappeared.

Free from the wind, the nets flew at the group at full speed.

But Billy had an idea. 'Midnight! Do the thing! The invisibility thing!'

Midnight looked panicked. 'I don't know if it works in daylight! I make things dark!'

'You have to try!' said Charlotte desperately.

'I believe in you, Midnight,' said Jordan. 'You've levelled up now with our bond, remember!'

'Everyone, get close to me!' shouted Midnight. She scrunched her eyes tightly shut in concentration. The rest of the dragons drew near to her and then, for a brief moment, her horns glowed, before a black cloud erupted from their tips, enveloping everyone in darkness. A bright flash followed, so bright Billy had to close his eyes, and when he opened them he gasped.

Midnight had done it. Billy could see there was a semi-transparent bubble surrounding them. They were floating in a cloud of invisibility.

Helicopters Vs Dragons

'Everyone, drop down!' yelled Billy. The group followed his instruction, dodging out of the way so the nets flew straight over them.

'Well done, Midnight!' said Thunder.

'You did it!' cried Billy.

'I knew you could,' said Jordan proudly.

Midnight was trembling with effort and didn't reply. She simply nodded and gritted her teeth with the exertion of keeping the invisibility cloud up.

'I am proud of you, Midnight,' said Lightning before her face hardened. 'We must fight back.'

'I do not want to attack the humans if we can avoid it,' said Tank.

'But it looks as if we might not be able to avoid it. They are attacking us!' said Xing.

'We need to focus on finding Frank and the sword,' said Spark. 'We must stop him from growing in power and making any more cuts between the realms. It is causing great instability in the Dragon Realm, and I fear the disastrous impact it will have on the Human Realm too.'

'What is his interest in dragons?' said Lightning.

Professor Edwards shook her head. 'I think dragons in this world are ... an unintended consequence of Frank's actions. But he will see you all as another means to gaining power. If he can control dragons, and if he is able to directly access the Forbidden Fountain, he will be unstoppable.' She took a deep breath. 'I have to go to the TURBO headquarters to shut down all the labs. It's the one thing I can do to slow Frank down. And I can try to find the golden elixir he's hidden away before he uses more on himself or it falls into the wrong hands.'

'What if Frank is there? You cannot face him on your own, not if he has the sword,' said Thunder, his eyes blazing. 'I will go with you. We will burn down his labs until nothing is left.'

'We should not harm any humans if we do not have to,' repeated Tank. 'Violence will only make things worse. It will encourage the humans to fight back harder, which will cause more dragons to attack. Everyone loses in this scenario.'

'You're right,' said Professor Edwards. 'As much as I would love to burn down all of TURBO, it won't help anyone. The best thing for me to do is focus on finding the golden elixir and trying to figure out what Frank's next move is. I know my way around TURBO and I'll do my best to avoid Frank.'

'But, Mum, will you be okay by yourself?' said Jordan. 'Maybe I should go with you. Me and Midnight.'

'I don't believe I'm saying this, but I think you're safer here with the dragons than you would be with me at TURBO,' said Professor Edwards with a sad smile. 'Oh, Jordan. I'm sorry for the mess I've got us into.'

'Nah, Mum, you have nothing to be sorry for. You were just doing your job – doing something you love. You couldn't have known that this Frank guy was such bad news when he hired you. You've been trying to make it right ever since you found out what he was up to, and I promise you, we *will* make it right.'

'When did you get so wise?' said Professor Edwards with a laugh.

Jordan grinned. 'Probably around the time I realized I had to come and save you.'

Billy felt a pang seeing Jordan and his mom interact, and suddenly he desperately wanted to be home in California to make sure his mom was all right. He wanted her to be proud of him too. There was a part of him that was strangely jealous of Jordan too. His mom was already deeply entrenched in this world and it didn't require any explanations.

Professor Edwards looked down at the River Thames far below them. 'There's a secret entrance to the headquarters in the river. Thunder, could you drop me off down there?' She pointed to her watch. 'This is a TURBO watch that gives me access into the building.'

'Of course,' said Thunder. 'We will go quickly to avoid any dragons or humans attacking us.'

'Be careful, Mum!' cried Jordan.

'You too,' she said. She looked at the rest of the children. 'All of you.'

Then Thunder and Professor Edwards soared out of Midnight's bubble and into the sky, heading towards the Thames.

'We must come up with a plan. If Frank is able to—' Spark began, but she was interrupted by another mighty *boom*.

Three more islands appeared above them. They hovered for a moment before falling out of the sky.

'Watch out! Get out of the way!' cried someone from below as the islands crashed around them. The dragons who had come into the realm dodged the falling islands with ease.

Thunder burst back into the invisibility cloud. 'I have dropped your mother off safely,' he said to Jordan. 'I would have joined her in her quest to gather more information, but I was far too large, and too conspicuous, to fit into the passageway that led to TURBO. I trust she will be all right. She seems a remarkably capable human.' Then he turned to the others. 'Things are getting even worse out there.'

Spark shuddered, her face serious. 'I fear we may

be past the point of no return. With all the cuts and portals Frank has created, the fabric that separates the realms is disintegrating. The Dragon Realm is collapsing into the Human Realm. What started as a trickle has now turned into a flood, and it is one that we may not be able to stop.'

'We have to try!' cried Billy. He felt desperate and terrified but he knew they couldn't give up.

'Of course the big question is: how do we do anything without the humans trying to kill or capture us?' said Xing. 'This whole experience reminds me why I prefer to stay in our own realm.'

'I do not know if there will be anything to return to in own realm after this,' said Spark softly.

Before Billy could register Spark's words, there was a loud commotion just outside their bubble. Four more helicopters had joined the first three, and there were other dragons flying around now too. Billy watched with horror as the helicopters started firing net after net after net.

Suddenly Midnight began shaking all over. 'I can't keep this up for much longer!' she burst out.

'On the count of three, Midnight, let down your

shield. I will take it from there,' said Lightning. 'But, Lola, I do not know if you will be able to hold on while I battle the helicopters.'

'I can carry Lola,' said Spark. Billy helped Lola off Lightning's back and onto Spark's.

'There are five helicopters,' said Thunder to Lightning. 'Are you sure you know what you are doing?'

'Do not worry,' said Lightning. 'I have a plan. Those helicopters will soon think twice before they try to bring down another dragon.'

'And you have us for backup,' said Xing.

'Spark?' said Billy. 'What do we do?'

'We will look for Frank in case he is not at the TURBO headquarters. But I am in your world now and I need your help, and Lola's, to guide me,' said Spark.

'I'll try to heal as many humans and dragons as I can,' said Buttons. 'Dylan can help me with his power of charm to try to convince the humans that we're not evil.'

'Ling-Fei and I will attempt to convince any rogue dragons to stop making things worse,' said Xing.

'Look at that one there, breathing fire all over the place. That is not helping anyone.'

'I will help Lightning,' said Thunder.

'And Midnight and I will be wherever we're needed!' said Jordan.

'Then we all know what we are doing,' said Tank. 'Charlotte and I will try to reason with any dragons we can, as well as save any humans who are caught in a dragon's line of fire.'

'Okay, Midnight, on the count of three, remember? One, two, THREE!' cried Lightning.

Midnight dropped her shield, and within seconds, all chaos broke loose.

Thunder and Lightning knocked the nearest helicopters out of the sky, and they plunged into the Thames below, sending huge waves of water crashing onto the pavements.

There were dragons battling everywhere. Xing and Midnight tried to stop them, but most were too angry that they were in the Human Realm to listen.

As Spark and Billy flew higher, trying to see if there was any sign of Frank, Tank and Charlotte soared up to meet them. 'The humans here do not seem interested in listening to us. They are more concerned with trying to catch us in those electric nets. Not that I blame them. That dragon over there just swallowed a car, for reasons I cannot fathom, and that one keeps ripping doors off buildings, seemingly for fun. Needless to say, it has not helped our cause.'

Suddenly, there was a roar so deep and so loud that it rattled Billy's bones.

'Is that dragon pushing the Shard over like a domino?' said Charlotte incredulously as the others turned and looked on in shock.

Then, just before the Shard crashed to the ground, the largest dragon Billy had ever seen swooped down and gripped the falling building with its giant claws, catching it in mid-air.

Billy stared at the royal purple dragon in awe. The dragon was *huge*.

'I didn't know a living thing could be *that* big,' muttered Jordan.

'Could it be . . . ?' said Thunder, studying the dragon.

'That is Gargantuan. Or Gar Gar for short. At least, that is the best human translation of his name. He is, as far as we know, the largest dragon to have ever existed,' said Tank.

'All brawn and no brain, as you humans would say,' sighed Xing.

'Garrrr,' roared Gar Gar. 'GAR GAR!'

The dragon flapped his wings furiously, wielding the Shard in front of him like a weapon.

The remaining helicopters turned to face Gar Gar and within moments more than a dozen nets were fired at the enormous dragon.

Gar Gar let out another bone-shaking roar and swung the Shard round in a wide circle, swatting the nets out of the sky like flies.

'I have not seen that dragon in over a thousand years. The last I heard, he got his head stuck in the Great Canyon in the Dragon Realm,' mused Tank. 'But I am pleased to see he has figured out an effective tactic to combat those nets.'

The helicopters fired another round of nets at Gar Gar, but he swatted them away again with ease. In retaliation, he roared and breathed out a tremendous blast of fire towards them.

One helicopter was set on fire and fell into the

Thames. The others came closer to Gar Gar, shooting out another round of nets.

There was a loud crackling as one of the pilots shouted into a megaphone out of his window. 'We have backup on the way. You cannot defeat us all. Give up now, or we will restrain every single one of you by force.'

Gar Gar let out what sounded like a chuckle. 'I will swat you out of the sky like I did your pathetic little nets!' With surprising quickness, the dragon burst towards the helicopters and swung the skyscraper in its claws, catching the tail of one helicopter. The helicopter spun wildly and started to fall from the sky.

'We have to save them!' said Ling-Fei, panic filling her voice.

'I agree. We cannot let innocent humans be harmed,' said Tank. 'Even if they are trying to harm us.'

Without warning, a fresh set of screams rang out from below. A group of dragons had started herding people into the Tower of London with their flames. Billy was certain that if they didn't step in, things would not end well.

He took charge. 'Tank, you and Charlotte go and

deal with those dragons by the Tower of London. Spark, Lola, Ling-Fei and Xing, let's try to stop Gar Gar from tearing down any more buildings.'

'I don't know how I can help with that, but I'll do my best!' said Lola.

Spark and Xing dodged helicopters and nets as they raced towards Gar Gar.

Xing flew directly into Gar Gar's face. 'Calm down, you big fool! You are making everything worse!'

'GAR GAR ANGRY!' roared Gar Gar. 'GAR GAR WANT TO GO HOME!'

'Yes, we know,' said Xing, as if she were speaking to a very small child. 'We are all angry, but you need to put down that building. The humans will just keep coming after us. Even though we are bigger and more powerful, we are outnumbered.'

Gar Gar suddenly noticed Ling-Fei on Xing's back.

'Human with you?' he growled, reaching out to swipe at Ling-Fei.

'Hey!' said Billy. 'Leave my friend alone!'

'Yeah!' cried Lola.

Billy urged Spark forward and Spark sent out her

own blast of electric power, blocking Gar Gar from reaching Xing and Ling-Fei.

Gar Gar howled in frustration as the electric current of Spark's blast shocked him.

'Put the building down, Gar Gar,' Spark said gently. 'And then you can take a rest. You must be very tired. We are going to fix this. I promise.'

Goldie flew out of Billy's pocket and went over to the giant dragon, squeaking in what Billy assumed was a reassuring manner.

'Flying pig is my friend!' said Gar Gar with delight. 'Hello, friend!' Then he sighed heavily. 'Gar Gar is tired. And hot. I like the river.'

'And you know what? I bet there are lots of shiny things hiding at the bottom of the River Thames,' Spark went on.

'Gar Gar likes shiny!'

'Yes, I know,' said Spark. 'All dragons like shiny things. Now put the building down. There you go.'

Gar Gar dropped the Shard without looking where it fell. Billy winced as he heard it fall onto the road below. Luckily all the humans had already evacuated the area, but it was still awful hearing the building hit the ground from such a height, flattening the surrounding buildings on impact.

Then something else caught Billy's eye.

'That's Frank's hovercraft!' he shouted, as he spotted the unmistakable sight of Frank Albert zooming through the sky. 'And he's headed towards Big Ben!'

'Gar Gar, you great oaf, we must be going. Remember, go and lie down in the river until this is all over,' said Xing, before racing after Frank's hovercraft.

'Come on, Spark!' cried Billy. He didn't know what Frank was doing, but he had a terrible feeling about it. Goldie squeaked and jumped back into Billy's pocket.

Suddenly, the bells of Big Ben's clock tower began to chime. But something was off about them; they were deafeningly loud and strangely tuneless. It felt as if the sound was drilling into Billy's brain and he resisted the urge to cover his ears, shaking his head to try to clear the noise instead. But they had bigger things to worry about.

'Let's go!' said Billy, determined to stay focused. 'We've got to catch Frank!'

With the sound of ringing bells echoing in the air, they raced towards Big Ben.

Battle at Big Ben

'To the clock tower!' cried Billy as they soared through the sky, the bells still clanging.

Thunder and Lightning clearly had the same idea, and they soon flew next to Spark as she followed Xing towards Big Ben – towards Frank Albert.

Tank, Buttons and Midnight weren't far behind.

'We're going to get him!' yelled Jordan.

Just then, the bells tolled so loudly that the entire clock tower shook and Billy could feel the sound reverberate in his bones. At the same moment, Billy felt a jolt run through Spark as if she had been struck. 'What is happening?' she cried out. Then her whole body went stiff and she fell from the sky like a rock, with Billy and Lola still on her back.

Next to them, all of the dragons began to fall.

'No!' Billy cried as they all tumbled through the air. He saw Tank's eyes rolling in his head as Charlotte desperately screamed in his ear. Buttons's entire body convulsed as it fell, and Dylan could barely hang on.

Billy pulled at Spark, trying to get her to wake up, to bring her back from wherever she had gone. *Spark! Spark! Stay with me!* Billy pleaded down their bond, but if Spark heard him, she didn't show it.

'We need to jump off!' Billy yelled, half pulling Lola to her feet on Spark's back. He looked at his friends and yelled as loudly as he could, 'WE HAVE TO JUMP INTO THE RIVER!'

Right before Spark hit the ground, Billy and Lola launched off the falling dragon and plunged into the River Thames. The other kids did the same, sinking deep into the murky water. They all came up a few moments later, spluttering and spitting out river water.

'Yuck,' said Lola, coughing out more water.

'Better the river than the pavement,' Billy said, more than a little relieved that his plan had saved them. He scanned the side of the river to find Spark. She had to be okay, she just had to be. And then he spotted her lying on the pavement, her tail dangling into the water. Billy swam over to her, his heart pounding. It wasn't the fall that he was worried about – Spark had fallen from much higher heights before and been fine – he was worried about whatever had taken over Spark's body as she continued to writhe on the ground.

With great effort, Billy and Lola hauled themselves out of the river and hurried to where Spark lay. The others pulled themselves up and went to their dragons. Midnight and Xing had landed closest to Big Ben's clock tower, narrowly missing knocking into it. The other dragons lay nearby, writhing and thrashing in pain.

Billy put a hand on Spark's side, and felt a surge of relief. She was breathing. That was a good sign. He tried to channel hope into her down their bond.

'Billy!' cried a voice from above. Billy glanced up and saw Jordan rushing towards him. 'Do you hear the ringing? I think Frank is doing something with the bells to hurt the dragons! Midnight managed to fly with me right next to the clock tower before she fell. We've got to get up there!'

'Whatever he's doing is causing them so much pain,' said Ling-Fei, practically in tears. 'We have to make it stop!'

Midnight's whole body was jolting up and down, as if controlled by invisible strings, and her horns flashed an angry red, like traffic lights.

Jordan's eyes were teary. 'I want to help her, but I don't know how!'

Billy tilted his head back and looked up at the clock tower. He knew what he had to do. He'd do anything to protect Spark. 'I have to go up there and stop those bells!' he said as he leaped onto the tower and started climbing it like a ladder. 'Keep an eye on our dragons, and keep a watch out for anyone who tries to come after me.' He took Goldie out of his pocket. The tiny gold flying pig was shivering. 'Goldie, you stay here with the others. Come and get me if anything happens!' Goldie squeaked and flew over to Dylan.

'Be careful, Billy!' cried Ling-Fei.

'If anyone can get up that tower, you can,' said Charlotte. 'We'll stay with the dragons!'

Helicopters were swirling around in the sky and Billy knew news cameras would almost certainly be trained on him, capturing his every movement. He imagined what his family would say if they saw him scaling Big Ben's clock tower, but he put the thought to the back of his mind. He had to concentrate on stopping the bells from ringing.

The bells tolled again as Billy reached the top of the clock tower and peered over the edge. Frank had taken one of the five large bells off its stand and was somehow cradling it under an arm. The *sanguinem gladio* was sheathed and strapped to his back, but Billy could still sense the magic radiating from it.

'Who do we have here?' said Frank, turning towards Billy. 'Aren't you one of those kids that was in the In-Between?'

'I'm here to stop you from hurting the dragons and messing with the realms,' said Billy, trying to sound as forceful as he could. He may not have his dragon by his side, but he still had his agility power, and his friends. Even if they were currently at the bottom of the tower. 'Whatever it is you're doing, stop now . . .'

He paused and tried to think of a way to sound more convincing. 'Or else!'

Frank let out a chuckle. 'Who do you think you are, kid? I don't take orders from anyone, and definitely not from a little boy.' He paused and studied Billy, sizing him up. 'And if anything, you should be thanking me. These dragons are dangerous. They aren't the oversized pets that fairy tales make them out to be. These are real, fire-breathing dragons that wouldn't think twice about having you as a snack.'

Frank pointed the large bell under his arm towards the sky, and Billy noticed for the first time that Frank's hands were not normal hands. They looked as if they were made of steel. Billy knew that he must have used more golden elixir on himself. Who knew how powerful he was now? Without warning, Frank struck the bell with his iron fist and somehow Billy could see the sound as it travelled out of the bell and across London. The sound of dragons crying out in pain mixed with the sound of the bell, and Billy glanced down, staring in horror as the dragons writhed on the ground.

'What are you doing?' Billy yelled. 'You have to

stop! Not all dragons are bad. There are good dragons that you're hurting. Good dragons that can help us bring peace and make things right again.' Billy wasn't sure if Frank fully understood all the chaos he was creating. Maybe he could get Frank to see how much harm he was causing and get him to change his mind.

'Go back home to your parents, little boy,' Frank said as he turned away from Billy and struck the bell again.

'I'm only going to ask you one more time,' Billy said, anger pulsing through him. 'Put down the bell, or I'll take it from you.'

Frank threw back his head and laughed, his whole body shaking. 'Oh, what an audacious boy you are! Such confidence! Such arrogance! You actually remind me of a younger version of myself.'

In that moment, Billy knew he wasn't going to get any further with Frank. As Frank finished speaking, Billy dashed across the tower using his super speed to kick the bell out of Frank's arms and through an opening in the tower. Now all he needed to do was grab the sword.

Frank gasped as the bell fell and smashed into

the pavement below, narrowly missing a dragon, before regaining his composure. 'Well, that was quite the nifty trick,' said Frank. 'Are you some sort of gymnast? It seems I may have underestimated you.' He gave Billy an evil grin. 'But I'm not someone who makes the same mistake twice.'

Frank shot his arm out towards one of the four remaining bells, and to Billy's surprise his arm stretched and stretched, as if it were made of elastic, and wrapped itself around the bell. Frank *definitely* had superpowers. He tore the bell from its stand and cradled it under his arm. 'Let's see how fast you really are.' Frank pointed the bell directly at Billy and pounded it with his free hand, over and over again, sending huge, visible shockwaves at Billy.

Billy dipped and dodged and bent in every direction around the bell tower, trying to avoid the soundwaves, but it was impossible. Frank hit Billy squarely in the chest with a blast and Billy felt as if his heart had stopped. Within seconds, he had collapsed to the ground.

Frank flashed his toothy grin and let out another chuckle. 'Well, that was fun. Goodbye, boy. A shame you were so insistent on battling me instead of joining me.' Frank paced over to Billy and held the bell directly over Billy's ear. He wound his fist up and Billy suddenly felt incredibly alone as he realized this might be it, the end, and he'd never see his family, friends or his dragon again. Terror washed over him and he closed his eyes as Frank's superpowered fist flew towards the bell.

Dragon Rising

Billy braced himself for the worst. But nothing came. He opened his eyes and saw Frank frozen in place, his eyes wide and mouth ajar.

And then Billy felt it – a tremendous rush of power vibrating through the air in a whirling tunnel. It was the same feeling he'd had when he'd been surfing in the ocean at his secret cove and saw the sea dragon. But this time the wave of energy was directed at the bells and at Frank, and it had frozen him in place. The energy blast stopped as quickly as it had started, but Frank stayed frozen. And then it was followed by a tremendous roar that rattled the entire tower.

Spark's voice echoed in Billy's head, weak but there.

Billy, be careful. She wants to destroy all the humans for what Frank has done. She? Who was she? Was the Dragon of Death back? Billy pulled himself up to look over the edge of the clock tower and gasped.

It was the sea dragon. But unlike the other dragons who were still writhing, she was rising up out of the River Thames, her huge neck unfurling more and more, until her body emerged, covered in barnacles and dark teal scales. She rose up on huge back haunches and suddenly she was at eye level with Big Ben . . . with Billy.

She was huge. Bigger than Tank. Bigger than any dragon Billy had ever seen other than Gar Gar.

This was the dragon that Spark had just warned him about.

Billy bowed his head respectfully, his heart hammering in his chest.

'You again.' The sea dragon's voice was low and raspy. 'Why do I keep seeing you?'

Billy was suddenly aware of everything happening around him. There were helicopters and news cameras everywhere, people shouting from every angle, and on the ground military tanks had started rolling in. Strangest of all, in the midst of the helicopters, there was a floating orb almost like a blimp, and in the basket underneath it were people in dark blue suits, all waving at him, trying to get his attention. A helicopter flew closer and without breaking eye contact with Billy, the sea dragon whacked it out of the air, like a cat batting a toy.

'Answer the question, human boy, before I grow weary of waiting and swallow you whole.'

'I-I don't know,' Billy stammered. 'But I'm a friend. I promise. I want to help the dragons.'

The sea dragon threw back her tremendous head and laughed, showing rows and rows of jagged yellow teeth. Billy gulped.

'Help the dragons! A human wants to help the dragons!' She turned to gaze upon the destruction and chaos all around her. 'Humans do not help. Humans destroy. It is in their very nature. They have ruined the one world they have, with their polluting and their greed, and as if that was not enough, they have broken our world as well. The holes between our realms can never be mended. The Dragon Realm is collapsing into the Human Realm.

I did not think it was possible, but here we are. My home is gone and I can never return again. I blame humans. And if this is to become the new home of the dragons, then there can be no humans here.' She raised her voice and continued, 'My dragon brothers and sisters, we do not want to be here, but if we must, we will take this world for our own. We will recreate it as a world fit for dragons, and dragons alone.'

Billy tried to calm his pounding heart. The sea dragon was almost worse than the Dragon of Death! At least the Dragon of Death had wanted to keep humans around, even if just for her own use.

The sea dragon lowered her voice again and looked back at Billy. 'Do not be afraid, human boy, it will not hurt. I do this only because I have no choice. I take no pleasure in it.'

How had things come to this? This dragon was going to destroy the world, and Billy didn't know how to stop her.

Spark! Do something! Billy cried down their bond.

The sea dragon's large eyes lit up in interest. 'Who are you speaking to? I can almost hear your thoughts they are so loud.' Then she gazed down at the dragons far beneath her. They were still incapacitated, but no longer writhing in pain. 'You are trying to communicate with a dragon down there! Are you a heart-bonded human? How extraordinary. Perhaps you do want to help the dragons.'

'How could you hear me?' Billy hoped that if he kept the sea dragon talking, maybe he could convince her *not* to destroy all humans.

'Correction. I cannot hear you, I can simply tell that you are trying to communicate. I can hear . . . the effort. It is the same reason that I am immune to the pain blast that the greedy human behind you created. I am a Sonic Dragon. I control and manipulate sound and energy waves, which is what that human was doing on an extreme level, but it does not affect me. My hearing is so astute that I can sense all kinds of energy and sound waves. When you try to speak to your dragon, it emits a wave that I can sense, even if I cannot hear what you are saying.'

'Wow,' Billy said, and he meant it. He was seriously impressed by that. 'Can I ask you one more question?'

'I suppose,' said the sea dragon, batting away

another helicopter that had come too close. 'It will probably be the last thing you do.'

'What were you shooting at before? When I first saw you on the beach?'

'I was attempting to close a portal that had opened between our realms – one that was sliced open by that sword. A sword that no human should have. Ever since I found myself in your realm, I have been attempting to close the holes between our realms. But soon I realized they cannot be closed once they have been opened. That is why things from the Dragon Realm keep falling into this world. Everything is unbalanced. That fool has broken both worlds more than he can comprehend.' The sea dragon took a deep breath. 'I grow tired now. I want to return to the sea in peace. I am sorry, but I see no other way.'

'There's always another way!' said a voice behind Billy. 'Humans aren't all like Frank. Some of us want to fix things. And if this is the new world, well, then we have the chance to build something better!'

Billy snapped his head round at the new voice. Lola stood, breathing heavily, at the top of the tower.

And next to her were Charlotte, Dylan, Ling-Fei and Jordan.

Billy had never been so glad to see his friends. 'How did you guys get up here?'

'Midnight was the first to come to after the bells stopped chiming and she flew us up here,' said Jordan, pointing to where Midnight now perched on the side of the clock tower.

'Thank goodness. There's no way I could have climbed this thing,' said Dylan. He waved at the sea dragon. 'I heard your big speech, and I have to say, I think you're being a bit hasty there.'

The sea dragon blinked. 'More human children? Daring to face me head on? How extraordinary.'

'Why are our other dragons still unable to move?' demanded Charlotte. 'Please release them!'

'That is not my doing. I have paused the sound bomb from the bells, but the dragons are still weak. They will recover soon, however you will not be here to see it.'

'But they aren't in pain?' said Ling-Fei anxiously.

'No,' said the sea dragon. 'How surprising that you care about them so much.'

'Of course we care,' said Charlotte. 'They're our dragons!'

Seeing his friends, old and new, gave Billy the rush of hope that he needed. He looked back at them. 'Thanks for coming, guys.'

'Just going to grab this thing while we're up here,' said Jordan, and he yanked the sword off Frank's back, who was still frozen to the spot.

'Careful!' said the sea dragon. 'That sword is more powerful than your human brain can comprehend.'

Lola stared hard at the sea dragon. Suddenly, she stepped forward from the group and walked past Billy, until she was so close to the sea dragon that they were almost nose to nose. Billy was vaguely aware of a helicopter coming in close, but this time the sea dragon didn't bat it away. 'I don't think you want to wipe out all the humans,' said Lola. 'You're good. I can sense it. I can't explain how, but I know.'

The sea dragon stared back at Lola. 'Why do you smell like the sea?'

Lola laughed, the sound bright and unexpected. 'Probably because I practically live in the sea. And you aren't wrong – humans do destroy things. The ocean is dying because of humans, but some of us want to save it. And in this new world, working together with the dragons, we can. The world isn't dying, it's beginning again.'

The sea dragon tilted its head to the side. 'Child, are you not afraid of me?'

Lola shook her head. 'No. I don't know why, but I'm not.' She laughed again. 'I was when I first saw you at the beach, but not any more.'

The sea dragon seemed to contemplate deeply. 'Perhaps I will save the six of you.'

'You have to save our families too,' said Charlotte.

'Fine,' said the sea dragon. 'As long as it's only a few.'

'I know you don't want to do this,' urged Lola again. 'Let us show you that we can be good.'

'That man is not good,' said the sea dragon, eyeing Frank. 'He is trying with every ounce of his being to get out of my control, but he cannot. Even with his ill-gotten power that he has been stealing from the In-Between.'

'You can do what you like with Frank,' said Billy quickly, 'but Lola is right. Humans aren't all bad.'

'And we can lead the way to the new world!' said Ling-Fei.

'Please,' added Dylan.

Lola very tentatively reached out and put her hand on top of the sea dragon's snout. 'We won't let you down.'

Billy gasped as he saw a burst of gold begin to glow from the sea dragon's heart. This was Lola's heart bond dragon? This giant sea monster dragon? How could it be?

But the heart bond could not be denied. The golden glow ran from the sea dragon to Lola's heart. Billy tensed, waiting to see what the sea dragon would do.

'Very well,' said the sea dragon. 'It seems I trust you.'

Lola beamed at the giant dragon. 'That's lucky,' she said, 'because I feel the same way about you! Now . . . how do you feel about the name Neptune?'

'It will do,' said the sea dragon. 'It will do.'

The Forbidden Fountain

Suddenly there was a huge cry of joy from the streets below. Billy realized that while the dragons had been incapacitated, hundreds and hundreds of people had come to the streets and had gathered around the Big Ben clock tower and the Houses of Parliament, watching the drama unfold above, thanks to the news cameras that had managed to capture everything. The military had put down their weapons and some people had started to bring the still-subdued dragons water in an attempt to comfort them.

Neptune gazed around at the sound of cheering. 'Why are the humans celebrating?'

'Because you just said you aren't going to destroy all

of humanity,' said Dylan. 'That's a pretty good reason for celebrating, if you ask me!'

'Hmph,' said Neptune. 'I hope I do not regret this.'

'Humans can surprise you,' said a new voice. A voice that made Billy's heart leap.

'Spark!' Spark was flying next to the clock tower, eyes and antlers glowing gold. 'You're okay!'

'I am and so are all the dragons, thanks to Neptune stopping Frank.'

'And the humans will be okay too, thanks to you six convincing Neptune to spare them,' said Buttons, who had flown up behind Spark.

'The world is going to be very different,' said Spark, 'but I believe what Lola said. Together, we can build a new world. A better world for humans and dragons.'

'I will believe it when I see it,' said Neptune. 'But I am willing to try.' She turned her gaze away to look out across London, and Billy realized a split second before it happened what he was going to see when he turned his head.

'Neptune! Frank is free!' Billy cried out.

Frank had taken advantage of Neptune's distraction and had somehow broken out of the frozen hold she'd had on him. 'What a load of baloney,' he said, shooting out his super-strech arm and grabbing the sword from a stunned Jordan. 'Working together to build a better world? The very thought makes me sick. Dragons are to be controlled, like any beast! And children are to be obedient. I will rule over all.'

Neptune turned, opening her mouth to send out a sonic blast, but Frank was too fast.

Billy watched in disbelief as Frank dived from the clock tower and disappeared into the River Thames. After everything they had done, he was going to get away with the sword. Who knew how many more cuts he would make, or how much more the realms could handle before everything fell apart? Billy had to stop him. Before he could think twice about it, Billy used his agility powers to dive into the River Thames after Frank Albert. He heard his friends cheering as he did.

The water was rougher than Billy expected. And murkier. He tried to stay calm as he looked around for Frank, but all he could see was the rush of air bubbles from his dive into the water. Then he spotted him. Frank was about fifty metres away and he appeared to be pushing buttons on the buckle of his belt.

Billy swam closer to Frank, careful not to be seen, but knowing he had to keep close or Frank would get away. With his enhanced agility and speed, Billy could move almost effortlessly through the water despite the strength of the current.

As Billy watched, he saw Frank detach the buckle from his belt and put it to his mouth. Was he somehow going to use it as a mouthpiece so he could breathe underwater? Would Billy have enough air to follow Frank wherever he was going? Billy pushed down the panic rising in his chest. He'd always been proud of how long he could hold his breath, but he'd never thought it would be a skill that he'd actually need to use.

Frank took the strap of the belt and pulled it taught. When he let go of it, the strap stayed straight and rigid. He broke the rigid strap in half and attached one piece to the bottom of each shoe as if they were propellers. Was Frank turning himself into some sort of impromptu boat? Billy swam faster towards him, anxious that Frank might be about to speed off at any moment.

Billy was only ten metres away when the makeshift

propellers swirled to life, pushing Frank like a missile through the water. Luckily, Frank still hadn't seen Billy, and with his super speed, Billy had managed to catch up to Frank and swim in his slipstream, which made it much easier to keep up with him. But it still took all of Billy's focus to stay behind Frank.

They had been travelling upstream like this for a hundred metres or so when Billy started to feel the burn in his chest. What started as an uncomfortable tingling quickly turned into a painful throbbing, like his lungs were on fire. Still he pushed harder. He couldn't risk going up for air and losing sight of Frank.

But as hard as Billy pushed, the distance between him and Frank grew, and with dismay Billy felt himself fall out of Frank's slipstream. The TURBO boss raced forward, leaving Billy behind. Billy pumped his arms as hard as he could, but he couldn't catch back up. His body was weak and he was out of air.

As he was about to give up, Billy saw Frank veer off to one side of the river and enter what looked like a secret passage in the muddy riverside wall and disappear. Steeling his nerves, Billy continued to move his arms and legs, pushing himself through the water. White spots appeared at the edges of his vision and the fire in his chest spread through his entire body, but still he kicked and kicked, until finally he found the secret door that had opened for Frank at the side of the river. He lunged forward and through the door just before it closed.

The door slammed shut behind him with a dull thud. Horror filled Billy as he realized he was still submerged. Was he trapped in an underwater tunnel? He was sure he didn't have a single breath of air left in his body and he didn't think he could swim any further. Half-conscious and on the last glimmer of hope, Billy swam up to the surface of the water and hoped there was air on the other side. Up and up he went, headfirst, until ... *bump.* The top of his head hit solid rock. Fear consumed Billy and he tried to work out what options he had. He reached his hands up above him to the water's surface, looking for a way out, and as he did, he realized that there was a sliver of air between the water's surface and the rock. It was too slim to fit his entire head, but if he went up face first, he would be able to get his nose and mouth above water. Billy thrashed upwards again until his face broke the surface, and he gulped down air with more vigour than he'd ever done anything else in his life. Billy allowed himself a long moment to catch his breath. *That was close*, he thought, when he heard Spark through their bond.

Billy! Billy! Are you okay?

Billy was grateful to hear Spark's comforting voice in his head. He was also grateful he didn't have to use any of his breath to reply. *Yes. It was close, but I managed to follow Frank into some sort of secret underwater tunnel. I think it must be the entrance to the TURBO offices that Professor Edwards mentioned earlier.*

Be careful, Billy. Stay where you are. We will try to find you.

There isn't time. I need to find a way to stop Frank before he does any more damage to the realms. I'm about a couple of football fields upstream from Big Ben. The secret passage is on the right side of the river wall. I'll keep looking for Frank.

Billy allowed himself a few more moments to catch his breath before plunging back into the water. Where had Frank gone? Billy scanned the underwater tunnel for clues, but the only light down there was coming from the faint glow of his super-suit. His eyes burned from the murky water. It was difficult to see and Billy couldn't make out any signs that Frank had been here. He went back up to the surface and took a deep breath before swimming deeper into the tunnel. He swam like this for a while, coming up for air every few metres and looking for anything that might tell him where Frank had gone, until he reached a dead end. Had he gone too far? Billy searched for a door or an opening, and to his surprise, the wall at the end of the tunnel slid open as soon as he approached it. Billy swam in and found he was in a small chamber. The door closed behind him, once again trapping him in a confined space underwater, but this time the water in the room emptied. When all the water had drained, a second door popped open, and Billy's heart skipped a beat.

'Professor Edwards!' said Billy. She was trapped in a glass enclosure to one side of the room, and on the other side was an oval-shaped glass pod with dozens of tubes coming out of it, connecting it to a large vessel filled with a golden liquid.

'What the heck is that thing?' said Billy.

'There's not much time to explain, Billy. We have to stop Frank! He found me in here searching for golden elixir, and he locked me in this enclosure. Now he's in that pod, pumping himself full of even more of the stuff. You have to destroy the vessel holding the liquid before Frank consumes too much of it and grows even more powerful!'

Billy dashed over to the tank with his super speed and pushed at the base of it with all his might. Slowly the tank began to teeter sideways until it tipped over completely and shattered onto the ground. But instead of spilling the golden elixir everywhere, the liquid vanished into nothingness as soon as the tank had broken.

'You monstrosity!' cried a voice from behind.

Billy whirled round to see Frank standing up in the pod.

'You've just destroyed the most valuable substance in this realm or any other!' Frank was filled with such anger that his eyes looked as if they might pop out and all the veins in his face bulged. 'Do you know what you've just done? You've *wasted* all of the golden elixir! Mark my words, you're going to pay for this!'

Frank unsheathed the sword that was still attached to his back and lunged at Billy, swinging it around wildly. Billy sidestepped the attack, tripping Frank as he passed and sending him barrelling into the wall.

'Oh, you little brat. This will be the last time I underestimate you,' said Frank as he held the sword with both hands in front of him. But instead of lunging at Billy this time, he swung the sword forward with his super-stretch arms, the blade moving at incredible speed towards Billy.

Billy flipped into the air, the sword just missing him.

A smile touched Frank's lips. 'Let's see how long you can keep that up for, little boy.'

Frank swung the sword like a propeller, slicing this way and that. Billy had to use all of his effort and concentration to dodge the attacks, jumping from wall to wall and floor to ceiling until Frank started to slow from the effort.

'Why won't you just hold still!' cried Frank as he swung another dozen sword strikes at Billy.

'Give it up, Frank,' said Billy. 'My clan of dragons

will be here any moment and you'll have no chance against all of us.' Billy was exaggerating, but he hoped it would convince Frank to give up.

Frank seemed to consider this before he gave Billy a wicked smile. 'Very well, boy. You may have won this round, but just you wait until I return!'

A second later, Frank slashed the sword through the air, creating a rip between realms, and then he disappeared into it.

Before Billy could second-guess himself, he jumped into the tear after Frank.

Going through a hole between realms was nothing like going through a portal. It felt more like falling down an endless black tunnel. Billy couldn't see anything, or feel anything, and if Spark or any of the others had arrived at TURBO and managed to follow him before the cut had closed, Billy didn't sense them.

He didn't know which way was up, or how long he fell for, but all of a sudden, he landed with a *thump*. Billy lay for a moment, catching his breath. It was still dark, but not pitch-black. There was a pulsing gold light coming from the centre of the damp, dark space he found himself in, and he could make out roots hanging from above, trailing over his body. He forced himself to his hands and knees and crawled towards the light. Where was he? And where was Frank?

As Billy got closer, he realized the light source was a tiered fountain of some kind, with gold liquid flowing from it. And then Billy spotted a figure kneeling at the fountain, drinking the gold liquid. It was Frank. The liquid glowed as it went down his throat, and Billy could see it as it spread through his body.

'The taste of pure power!' Frank cried. He twisted round towards Billy, and Billy gasped. For a moment, Frank's entire body had turned to steel, but then quickly returned to flesh again.

'I sensed that you'd followed me here. But now you don't have any dragon friends to protect you, I can finish you for good.'

'You said you wouldn't underestimate me,' said Billy, 'and yet you seem to be doing just that.' He sprang to his feet and did two flips in the air, kicking Frank away from the fountain. Gold liquid sprayed around them.

'Be careful!' Frank cried. 'Don't waste any of it!

That's the most powerful substance in any realm. I assume you got your little flipping and jumping power from one of those pearls? Where do you think the pearls came from? Or this sword? They came from here. From the Forbidden Fountain itself.'

Even though Billy already knew this from the dragons, hearing Frank say it sent a chill down his body. This was the kind of power that should not be toyed with.

'Don't look so surprised,' Frank said with a laugh. 'Yes, I know about your little magic pearls. I had an expert team of researchers working around the clock to find any kernel of truth in the outlandish tales I had heard. And that meddling Professor Edwards was one of the best. Dragons and portals are her area of expertise, and she knew all about the legend of the pearls too. Most people thought they were all fairy tales, but I knew they were true. And now I have the golden elixir running through my veins – the exact same substance that created your little magic pearl. You think you're powerful? That your dragons are strong? Well, nothing compares to me! Now that I've found the Forbidden Fountain, I plan to drink from it as often as I need, and grow more and more powerful with every sip! Who needs TURBO? Who needs anything? I, Frank Albert, will rule humans and dragons for eternity!' He smiled with manic glee and Billy felt horror wash over him at hearing the full extent of Frank's plan.

Billy, where are you? I sense so much darkness around you.

It was Spark, speaking through their bond. It even reached here, in the In-Between.

I'm at the Forbidden Fountain, Billy thought back. *Frank is drinking from it. Can you get here?*

I do not know how you reached it. It is hidden deep in the In-Between. I cannot find it, or you. And the liquid from the Forbidden Fountain is far too potent for any human or other being. Frank will become volatile and unpredictable. You must get the sword and come back as soon as you can. Take the sword, cut into the air and come through. Think of me and the others. We will be your guide.

What do I do about Frank?

Without the sword, he will be locked in the pocket of the In-Between with the Forbidden Fountain for ever. He will not survive.

Before Billy could respond, he saw a metal fist hurtling towards him. Quick as a flash, he flipped up and over Frank's attack.

'Oh, what a jumpy little jumping bean you are,' said Frank. 'It'll be a lot less effort for both of us if you just stay put. You don't stand a chance against me, so you might as well accept defeat.'

Frank threw a flurry of punches at Billy, stretching his arms across the In-Between. It took all of Billy's strength and agility to keep from getting hit. Frank was throwing so many punches it was as if he had a hundred arms.

'ARGH! Stay still, you little gnat, and let me squash you!' Frank took a step back and stretched his hands out on either side of him, before slamming his iron palms together in a thunderous *clap*. 'Dodge this!'

A giant sound wave swept towards Billy, rippling as it tore through the air. Billy sensed its direction and rolled on the ground beneath it, kicking out his legs as he did so and knocking Frank off balance.

The sword fell off his back and, in one swift movement, Billy snatched it up off the ground.

'GIVE THAT BACK TO ME!' cried Frank, lunging for Billy.

Billy unsheathed the sword and swung it in an arc in front of him. 'Get back!' he yelled. The sword was heavier and more unwieldly than it looked, and he staggered forward. The sword *swooshed* in front of him and sliced through the base of the Forbidden Fountain. It toppled over, and gold liquid gushed everywhere.

'NO!' screamed Frank. He sank to his knees in it, trying to collect as much elixir as he could.

Billy scrambled back to avoid the gushing gold, and lifted the sword again, slicing into the air like Spark had told him. All around him, the ground was shaking and cracks began to form, gold liquid spilling into the cracks. Billy grabbed one of the roots hanging above them and hoisted himself up, avoiding the flowing liquid.

'You don't know what you've done!' shrieked Frank. He tried to stand but his body had turned to steel again, and this time it stayed like that. Gold began to pour out of his nose and ears and mouth, as if he was turning into some twisted version of the Forbidden Fountain itself.

Billy sliced at the air again, desperate to get out

of there, desperate to leave Frank and the Forbidden Fountain behind. This time a hole opened up, and he could have sworn he heard Spark's voice crying out to him. Billy glanced back. The golden liquid was flowing faster now, gushing and rising. It was up to Frank's chest and he stood there unmoving.

Billy paused, wanting to help him. Drowning in a fountain of magic gold was not a fate he would wish on anyone, even Frank Albert. But then another crack opened up in the ground, and the steel Frank, gold river and what was left of the Forbidden Fountain fell into it, leaving Billy swinging on the roots above.

With as much energy as he could muster, Billy swung himself, and the sword, into the hole he had cut in the air, and flung himself out of the In-Between.

A New World

Billy fell through the hole between realms and burst into the sky above London. Then he plummeted towards the ground, spinning head over toe, gripping the sword for dear life.

SPARK! WHERE ARE YOU?

And then Spark was there, grabbing him with her talons and carrying him back to Big Ben, where his friends and their dragons were waiting.

'Here's the sword,' Billy said, swaying on his feet as handed it over to Tank.

'And Frank?' said Jordan uneasily.

'We don't have to worry about him any more,' said Billy. He tried to say something else but his mouth felt as if it was full of cotton, and his eyes were heavy. He heard Buttons speak, but it sounded as if it came from far away.

'He was in the In-Between for too long,' said Buttons. 'He's gravely unwell. Spark, hold him, and I'll try to heal him.'

Secure in the knowledge that he was with Spark, and his friends, and that at least for the moment he was safe, Billy closed his eyes, and let the darkness take him.

When Billy woke, he was in a big, fluffy bed, in an enormous room with a chandelier hanging from the ceiling. A room so big that Spark could fit in it. 'Hello, Billy.'

'Billy!' Charlotte, Dylan, Ling-Fei, Lola and Jordan rushed towards him. 'You're awake!'

'Do not crowd him! For goodness' sake, give him some air.' Billy recognized Buttons's voice. He was there too, fussing next to him.

'Where ... where are we?' said Billy, sitting up against the extremely fluffy and comfortable pillows.

A huge grin split across Jordan's face. 'Mate, we're in Buckingham Palace.'

'WHAT?'

'Everyone, like everyone in the entire world, saw what happened at the clock tower. They saw Lola get Neptune onside and they saw you go after Frank. Top officials at TURBO admitted what Frank was really doing. The company has been disbanded, and loads of researchers who worked there, like my mum, are coming forward.'

'And there's this secret organization, although I guess not so secret any more, who know about dragons! And all kinds of other supernatural things! They want to work with us!' said Charlotte. 'Because guess who are suddenly the world experts in dragons?' She bounced on her feet, too excited to not answer her own question. 'We are!'

'We're heroes, apparently,' said Dylan. 'Which is why they've put us up in Buckingham Palace. Plus, this was the only place with rooms big enough for the dragons too.'

'Not all the dragons,' said Lola. 'There's no way Neptune could fit in here.'

Billy's head spun. 'How long have I been out for?'

'Just a day. Your parents are on their way. They saw

everything! Spark offered to fly them here via portal, but they said they'd rather take a plane,' said Lola.

Billy turned to Spark. 'You went to my house?'

'It seemed wise that someone should check on your family. Your brother, Eddie, is a dragon fan, you know. He was very helpful in keeping your mother calm while I explained everything.'

Just then, there was a loud crash outside, followed by a shout.

Ling-Fei glanced out of the window. 'Just a peach tree,' she said. Then she turned to Billy. 'Dragon Realm is still collapsing into this world. There doesn't seem to be any way to stop it. Neptune was right – there really is no going back there.'

Billy gazed at all of his friends. He'd never thought that anyone would understand what had happened this summer, but now they had Jordan and Lola too. And the whole world knew about dragons! Everything had changed. 'So ... what happens now?'

'Now we do what we said we would do. We work with the dragons to build a new world,' said Lola. 'One that's better for everyone.'

'Everyone is counting on us,' added Charlotte.

'But we're just kids,' said Billy.

'Kids with dragons. Kids who saved the world. On TV, with everyone watching,' said Dylan.

'You *can* do this, Billy. You all can. And we will be by your side,' said Spark.

His friends and the dragons all looked at him expectantly. The Thunder Clan was there too, and then Billy saw Goldie on Lightning's shoulder, and he broke into a wide grin.

'You're right,' he said. 'We've got this.' He didn't know what the future held, but he did know that whatever happened, he could face it, because he had his friends, and his dragon, by his side.

ACKNOWLEDGEMENTS

Thank you for coming along with us on a new Dragon Realm adventure! The only reason we're able to keep writing Dragon Realm stories is because people keep reading them – so our first thank you is to you, the reader.

Thank you as always to our incredible Dragon Dream Team. To our agent, Claire Wilson, who is always excited for a new dragon book and always believes in us. Shout-out as well to Tom and Oly – we are so glad you like the books! And thank you to the rest of the team at RCW, especially Safae El-Ouahabi and Sam Coates.

To the incomparable Rachel Denwood for leading Team Dragon to new heights – we are so glad we get to work with you.

Thank you to the amazing Amina Youssef for your enthusiasm and editorial brilliance.

And thank you to our copyeditor, Catherine Coe, for being the best copyeditor any author could ask for, and to our proofreader, Leena Lane, for her eagle-eyed expertise.

The Dragon Realm book covers are truly a work of art, and for that we have to thank Jesse Green in design and, of course, the ridiculously talented Petur Antonsson for the cover and chapter heading illustrations. We couldn't have dreamed up more perfect covers for the books! Thank you for bringing our dragons to life in such stunning style.

The sales, marketing and PR teams at Simon & Schuster blow us away with their brilliance. Thank you to everyone in the teams, but especially Laura Hough, Dani Wilson, Sarah Macmillan, Ian Lamb, Dan Fricker, Sarah Garmston, Eve Wersocki Morris and Louisa Danquah for all of their hard work on the series.

The audiobooks are fantastic (we really recommend them!) – thank you to Dominic Brendon at Simon & Schuster and our narrator Kevin Shen for making them so epic.

We are incredibly grateful to booksellers for being so amazing and always supporting the series! We'd like to especially thank Queens Park Books, Muswell Hill Children's Bookshop, Pickled Pepper Books, Chicken and Frog Bookshop, Stories by the Sea, Tales on Moon Lane and Waterstones for their support. Special shout-out to Laura-Jayne Ireton and Rhiannon Tripp for being such advocates for the books.

We also want to thank all the amazing teachers and librarians who have introduced the books to their students. You are heroes!

We are very lucky to have so many wonderful friends to cheer on our dragons – thank you to Cat, Kiran, Tom, Anna, Kate, Abi, Katherine, Roshani, Krystal, Alwyn and Samantha.

We'd also like to thank our friends Jeni, Maarten, Kris and Dyna, as well as their wonderful small humans.

And finally, to our wonderful family across the globe. A dragon-sized thank you to the Tsang, Webber, Hopper and Liu family members for their support and enthusiasm. Especially our parents and siblings.

And to our daughters, Evie and the newest tiny Tsang, Mira. We love you always.

KATIE & KEVIN TSANG met in 2008 while studying at the Chinese University of Hong Kong. Since then they have lived on three different continents and travelled to over 40 countries together. As well as the DRAGON REALM series, they are the co-writers of the young fiction series SAM WU IS NOT AFRAID (Egmont) and Katie also writes YA as Katherine Webber.

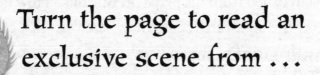

Turn the page to read an
exclusive scene from ...

DRAGON DESTINY

Coming September 2022!

The volcano rose up ahead of them, smoking ominously. It jutted out of the sea like a giant crooked tooth.

'Are we sure we have to look inside that thing?' Dylan called from his perch on Buttons. 'How do we know the bones are there? They weren't in that creepy cave that tried to swallow us.'

'Which is exactly why we have to look in the volcano,' said Billy, urging Spark on even faster. 'If the bones weren't in the cave, they must be here. I just have a feeling.'

'I hate when you get that kind of feeling,' said Dylan.

Billy grinned over his shoulder at his friend, and then saw something that made his blood run cold.

In the distance, the Dragons of Dawn were gaining on them. He recognized them by their orange and yellow glowing scales. Even though the Dragons of Dawn didn't know what Billy and his friends were looking for, they wanted to destroy the human children and their dragons. Because Billy and the others represented what the Dragons of Dawn hated most of all – peace between humans and dragons.

'We don't have much time!' cried Ling-Fei, who

had spotted the Dragons of Dawn at the same time as Billy. 'They're catching up!'

'We could always fight them off,' said Charlotte, brandishing a fist in the direction of the yellow and orange dragons. 'And then keep looking for the bones when we know they aren't on our tail.'

'There are too many of them,' said Spark. 'Even with our powers combined, I do not know if we could take on that many dragons.'

'But we could at least slow them down,' said Xing. 'We do not all need to go into the volcano.'

'Xing's right,' said Billy.

'Of course I am,' said Xing. 'I am always right.'

'So we divide up?' said Jordan, warily watching the rapidly approaching pack of dragons. 'Some of us go into the volcano, and some of us try to stop the Dragons of Dawn?'

'What a choice,' said Dylan dryly. 'Death by volcano fire, or by dragon fire.'

'Nobody is dying,' said Billy firmly. 'And I'm the only one going into that volcano.'

'What are you talking about?' said Lola. 'Now is not the time to be the hero!'

'I'm the only one who can!' said Billy. They were nearly at the mouth of the volcano, and the smoke was making his eyes sting. 'I can use my agility power to scale down inside of it and look for the bones. Xing and Ling-Fei can use their seeker magic to guide me, and the rest of you can distract the Dragons of Dawn.'

'I can help too!' squealed Midnight. 'I can use my power to hide the volcano while you're in there.'

'Great idea, Midnight,' said Jordan, beaming with pride at his dragon.

'Then it is settled,' Tank said in his low, rumbling voice. 'Billy will go into the volcano. Spark will keep watch from above, along with Midnight and Jordan and Xing and Ling-Fei will try to guide him. The rest of us will attempt to slow down the Dragons of Dawn. We will not be able to beat them, but we can at least keep them from discovering what we are after.'

'I bet we can beat them,' said Lola with a ferocious grin. 'Come on, Neptune! Why don't we go out and give them a big hello?' The huge sea dragon roared in approval and dove back into the ocean, with Lola still hanging on tight.

'Neptune will be able to stun them momentarily

with her sound blast, but the rest of us need to be ready to fight,' said Tank. 'Are you ready?'

'Always!' cried Charlotte. 'Come on!'

'Be careful in that volcano, Billy,' said Dylan anxiously, before he and Buttons flew in the direction of the Dragons of Dawn.

'I'll be fine,' said Billy, but he felt his throat go dry as he gazed down into the molten core of the volcano. He sure hoped the bones they were looking for really were in there.

'There is something in there,' said Xing. 'I can feel it.'

'Me too,' said Ling-Fei.

'We know that the first dragons came from volcanos,' said Spark. 'There had been nothing, and then there were dragons. And the very first one was . . .'

'Glorious Old,' murmured Billy. 'Who would have gone back to where she came from when she was hurt.'

'Not just hurt, but dying,' said Spark.

'And I only need one of her bones to summon her spirit?'

'So the stories say.'

Billy gulped. This was the best chance they had at finding the spirit of Glorious Old. The only chance. And without her help, all was lost.

Have you read?

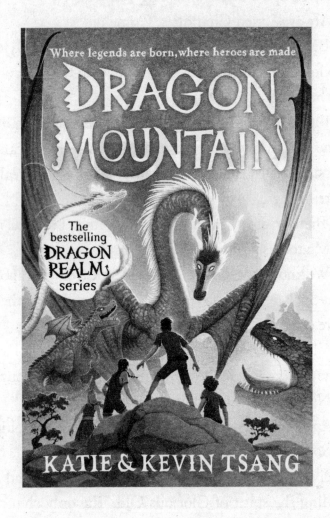

Have you read?

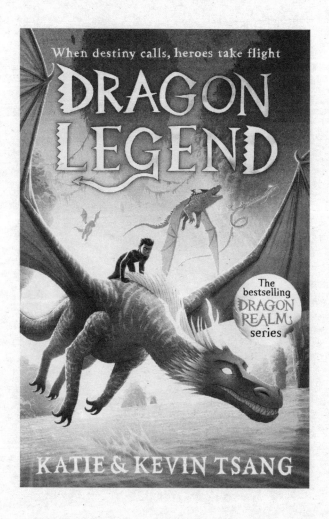

Have you read?

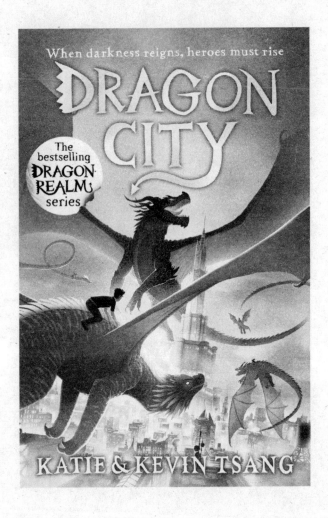